Startling
Sci-Fi

Startling Sci-Fi

edited by
Casey Ellis

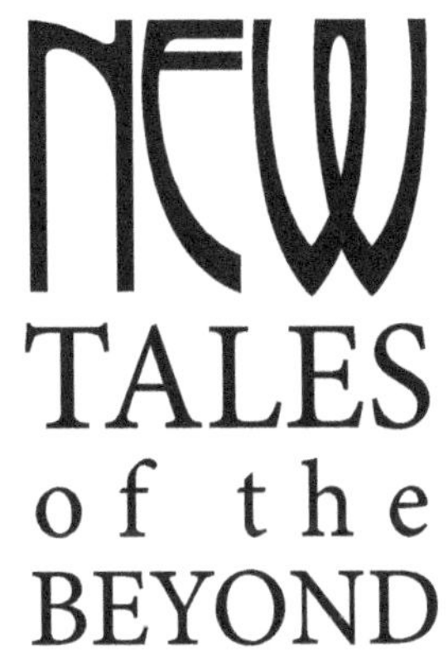

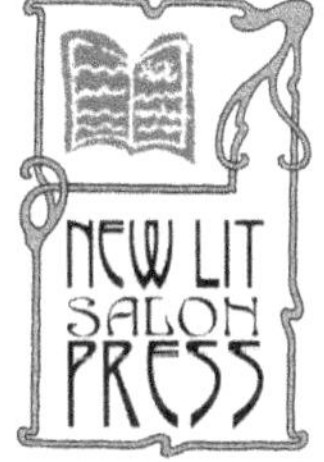

Also in the NEW series

Southern Gothic: New Tales of The South edited by Brian Centrone &
    Jordan M. Scoggins
Behind the Yellow Wallpaper: New Tales of Madness edited by Rose Yndigoyen

Other titles by New Lit Salon Press

I Voted for Biddy Schumacher: Mismatched Tales from the Mind of Brian Centrone
Retrospective by Michael Tice
Erotica by Brian Centrone
Salon Style: Fiction, Poetry & Art edited by Brian Centrone

Startling Sci-Fi: New Tales of the Beyond

Published by New Lit Salon Press, 2015

Edited by Casey Ellis
Editor-in-Chief, Brian Centrone
Line Edited by Karen Lea Siegel and Rose Yndigoyen
Art by Stefanie Masciandaro
Art Direction and Design by luke kurtis

"Crow Magnum Xix" was previously published in *Woolf Magazine*, ed. Jason Beech, Bloom & Curll Bookshop, Bristol, UK, September 2011

New Lit Salon Press
Carmel, NY

Print ISBN 978-0-9885512-9-9
eBook ISBN 978-0-9885512-8-2

www.newlitsalonpress.com

Table of Contents

Almost John

John

Scott Lambridis

The Peterson Center for Independent Living was built on top of the subway. Construction crews had fenced off the parking lot leading to the eastern entrance, which meant commuters like myself had to walk an extra five minutes across the street to the western entrance. The sign hung on the fence warned that it would take three, maybe four years to finish the Peterson Center. It was going to be a block-long multi-leveled complex with two levels above ground and who knows how many below.

I spent many walks calculating the accumulated time this diversion cost me, but after only two years the complex was complete and the fence around the parking lot leading to the eastern subway entrance was again unlocked. Only now this entrance took you right by the large windows of the Peterson Center before leading you down the stairs onto the train platform. On the other side of those windows, within a dizzying maze of ramps and conference rooms, were the cyborgs.

"They're not cyborgs," said Bill, "They're disabled. It's a conference center for the handicapped. Jesus, Mike, have a heart."

I nodded to Bill, as if I thought he was right.

Bill and I went to college together. Now we were neighbors. He worked from home but on Wednesdays he supervised the university computer lab, and since I commuted to the post office every day, we often found ourselves walking together to the subway on Wednesday mornings. We were both in a better mood now that we didn't have to cross the street to the other entrance.

As we approached the stairway we passed the Peterson Center's large windows. Of course they were cyborgs, I thought. They were somewhere inside, rolling about, up and down the ramps of their new conference center, but what they did in there, what they congregated about, I did not know. How could I prove it to Bill when the window revealed nothing?

Once, I'd stopped to tie my shoe beside those same windows, and when I stood up, I saw one. Through the glass, I saw his head and face and the collar of a red shirt. He was right there, looking out as I was looking in. We had caught each other's eye and for a moment I knew we both thought the same thing. For a moment we both believed we knew each other.

Oh look, there's my friend John, the painter, I thought. Same hair, same nose and cheeks, round and chubby with glasses—except wait, this one doesn't have any legs. It has only the tiniest of appendages you could barely call an arm, with cables running down it into a mess of other cables leading to a little stick on the armrest of a seated exoskeleton.

And my face must have been similar to one of his cyborg-friends' faces because his look was equally expecting—full of hopeful recognition and on that verge of excited surprise—only I couldn't be his friend because I was fit. I was locomoting on my own two feet, upright, unencumbered, symmetrical and one hundred percent organic.

"Not John," I said, "*Almost* John," and we both turned from the window.

The following Wednesday, the ramps and rooms behind those same windows were empty again as Bill and I passed. I told him about Almost John.

"The technology is amazing," I said. "They're so human-like." When I failed at describing what Almost John looked like (for Bill had never met the original), Bill suggested that next time I take a photo.

"Don't you wonder what they're planning in there, all by themselves?" I asked. "I've never seen a single non-cyborg inside. Not even one. The city must have a lot of trust in their good intentions."

"Mike, you're such an ass," said Bill. He insisted again that they weren't cyborgs. He said I was dangerously close to sounding like a racist.

But of course they were cyborgs. The exoskeletons gave it away. If you separated Almost John from his housing, the organic portion would die within a few days at most, flailing its one arm on the linoleum unless someone cared for him or replaced the chair.

And each exoskeleton was unique. If not completely individual, they were at least categorically varied, like species within a genus. Most of them had some sort of mechanical carriage on which the biological portion rested, secured by a variety of harnesses, straps, and clasps made from other, processed, biological materials.

The general population of cyborgs seemed to maintain an organic to mechanical ratio of about fifty-fifty, but as in any bell curve there were variants on both sides. I saw female ones who swung their hips just like us while something synthetic prevented their necks from lopping over to the side, or else they could swing their hips in place but when they walked they had to hunch over and use metal extensions to simulate their walking. And the rolling ones barely batted an eye at them when they passed.

There were other ones too—ones retaining only a slim percentage of biological material, like an eyeball, a face, or a reproductive organ. It was fastened down within a web of whirring mechanics, and it was difficult to imagine this slim sliver of organic matter provided any real source of sentience or agency. When these creatures came to the junctions between the ramps and had to slowly and tediously maneuver themselves around the corners, they showed no signs at all of hardship or joy.

If a couple of the mostly organic cyborgs (one of the ones retaining fully expressive mouths and eyes) happened to meet one of these mechanical wonders as they came around the corner, their expressions changed. They gave that same look of reverence a child gives to its decrepit elders. They slowed, almost to a stop, before continuing on, past that solemn and restrained thinker still trying to navigate the dreaded corner.

And then, last Tuesday, the complex lifted from the ground.

When it began, for a moment I wondered if there was an earthquake, or if there had been a collision of trains in the subway, but there was no mistaking the way the complex shook, and the way it inched up, scraping against the concrete around it. Inch by inch, it pulled itself from the ground, revealing not one or two, but three entire floors under the earth. The trains below were loud; the complex had formed one side of the subway, and debris showered the platforms. As the complex rose, it flipped up all the surrounding flowerbeds, and for a moment the remains of the fence around the parking lot hung down, until it ripped away and fell back to earth. Not a single window broke. The sign announcing the "Peterson Center for Independent Living" turned toward me as the complex slowly rotated.

Independent living indeed, I thought.

Now the complex was entirely detached from the earth. It was beautiful. Humming thrusters embedded somewhere within the bottom floors sent out a layer of fog, and the air had the blur of a gasoline mirage but there was barely any wind, and certainly not a bit of fire.

I watched from the sidewalk holding a half-eaten apple. I had never seen a spaceship before. It took less than a minute for the whole thing

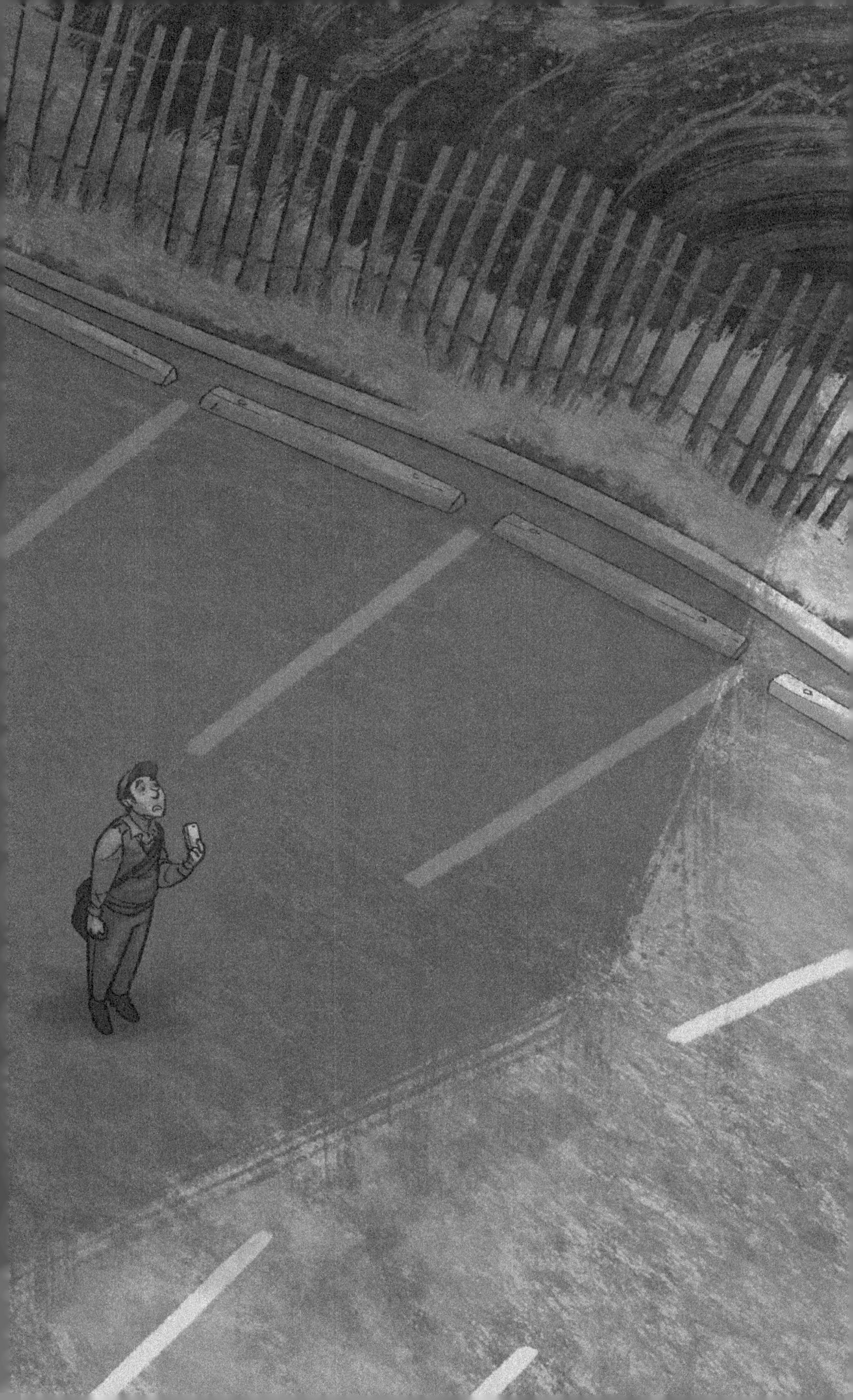

to lift off. I held up my phone. I wanted to take a picture. I couldn't wait to show Bill. Fucking cyborgs, I told you so, I thought as I framed the scene in my lens.

But the memory on my phone was full.

I stabbed at the buttons to clear up some space, but I couldn't decide what other photos to delete, what other memories: dinners with my girlfriend, Bill's new puppy, my birthday party at the post office. I didn't want to lose any of it, and by the time I looked back up the complex had accelerated.

And then, framed by one of those large windows, I saw Almost John again. There he was, looking just like my friend John, with that same nose and that same pair of glasses and those same round and chubby cheeks. This time he was too far above for me to see his wheelchair or that shrunken arm, but it was him. And I saw that he was smiling at me. He was looking down and smiling back at me. His face then twisted into a pitying bout of laughter.

Where, where were you going, Almost John? How did you do it? And why did you leave? I wondered then as I'm wondering now.

Almost John just kept laughing though, laughing until he was gone.

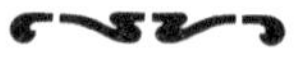

Embraced

Eve Fisher

That week's pilgrimage was the worst, and Tyra was in a foul mood when I brought her back home. I hurried her past Denis and Gleb and up to her bedroom where I fed her vodka, with enough bread so she wouldn't get sick. She was drunk a delightful two days. The third, she sobered up and said, "Let's go."

"Where?" I asked, putting on my clothes.

"What do you bloody well care?" She tied back her hair and put on her coat. "I want to see how far They've gotten."

It was a good trip. Ukrainian spring, sunshine and flowers by day, a crackling fire and Tyra at night. I enjoyed myself, even if there were ETs all the way to the Carpathians.

"Bloody everywhere," Tyra muttered. "Let's go to the Barrens."

Nearly there, and Tyra spotted him in the scrub, atop a hill, his back to us. And an ET, looming above him in a full twenty feet of sharp-bladed gold. The man scrambled back—not that it would do any good.

"He'll kill himself falling before It gets him," I commented. The man pulled out a weapon and sprayed something dark across the sky—and the ET collapsed. I was stunned speechless.

"Come on, Yuri," Tyra urged, and took off.

I raced after her. The man had slid over the hill, and Tyra followed. I crested and saw five headless bodies lying on the ground behind him, a wailing infant in the middle. Tyra called, "Good job," and he whirled towards her. I was ready to drop him if he made a move to hurt her.

"Peace, friend," Tyra said. "Anybody that can kill an ET is welcome here. What was it that you used?"

"Corrosive," he said.

"How do you make it?"

"I don't know," he said. "I just use it."

"Figures. How's the tyke?"

"It's crying."

"You have to hold them. Men." She handed me her gun and picked up the baby. "There, there," she said. "It's all right. No ET's going to get you today." The baby hushed in her arms. I came up next to her and she said, "Let's go."

We walked away. The man watched us, stunned, and then cried, "Where are you going?"

"East. You coming?"

He followed, of course.

"What was all that about?" he asked as we went back down the hill. "That thing…it was going to kill the baby."

I didn't tell him that whatever he used on It killed the adults.

"Worse," she said. "It was going to embrace it. Good God. You don't know what I'm talking about, do you?"

"No."

"You're from Outside."

"You're no Russian yourself."

"Quite true. Tyra Wilson from Perth. Married a Ukrainian bloke, moved to L'viv ten years ago now." She shifted the baby in her arms. "It's heavy. This here is Yuri Dzhankov. Who are you?"

"Paul Thompson. NATO Field Agent."

"There isn't any bloody NATO left."

"There isn't much of anything left," he admitted, "just titles."

"And wicked weapons. That corrosive, we've got to get some of that. Only stuff I've seen that'll wipe out an ET."

"What the hell is an ET?" he asked.

"You saw it. What do you think it was?"

"I don't know what I thought it was. Giant insect, mutant, alien, I don't know."

"Try the last."

"Tyra," I interrupted. "People."

We dropped to the ground behind a rocky knob.

"See them?" Tyra whispered. Mr. Thompson nodded. "Take a good hard look at them."

He looked. At first he saw nothing but a handful of people, relaxed and sitting in the sun, drinking and talking and… Then his eyes widened, and he started backing away instinctively. He had seen Them. Each and every person was interpenetrated by a many-planed, golden Thing, graven with dark lines that writhed and moved, towering in layered arcs and claws and blades and eyes.

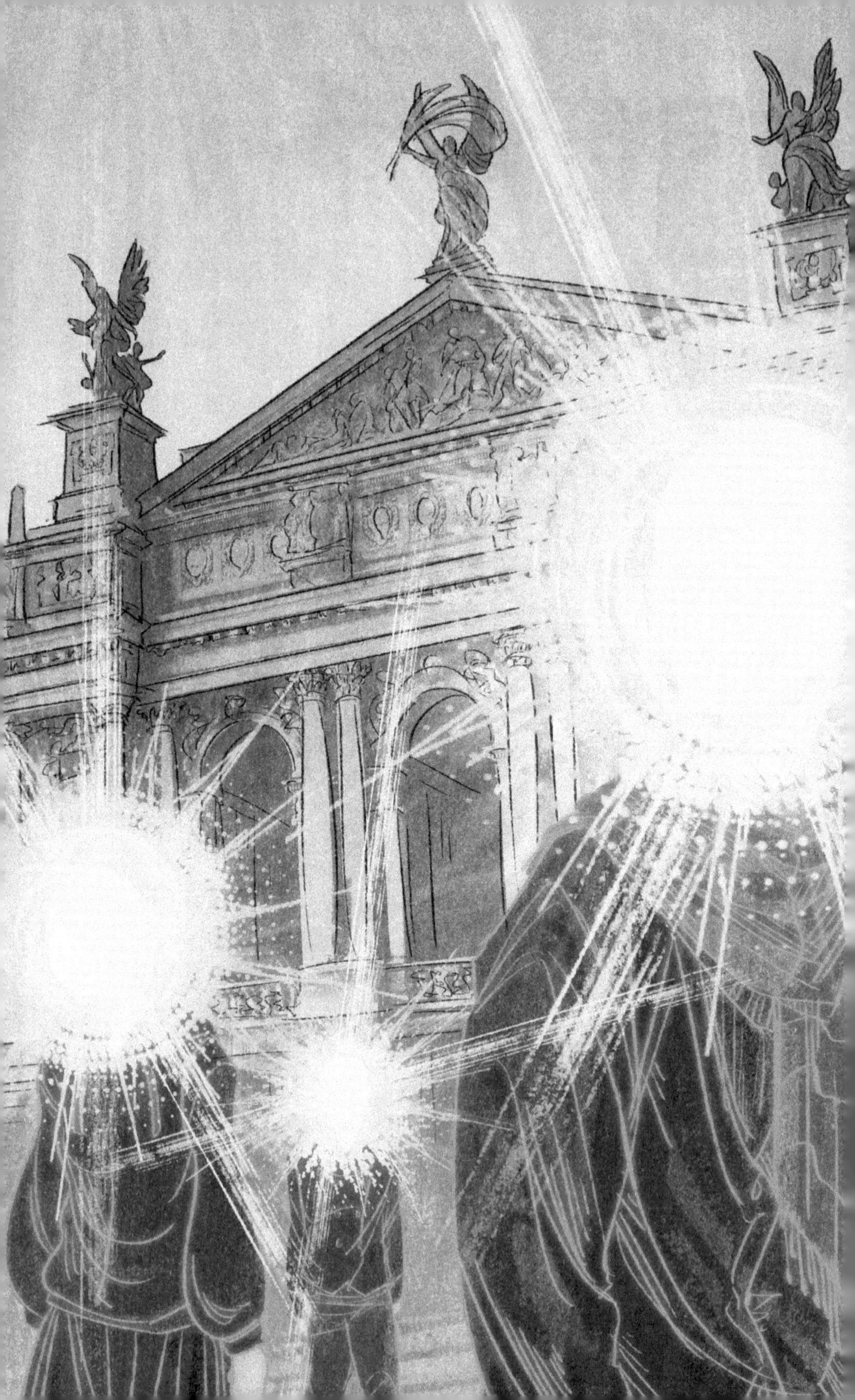

"Probably from her village," Tyra said. "The people you wiped took her out from here this morning and now everybody's waiting for them to come back. And every bloody one of them's been taken by an ET." She moved back away from the knob and said, "Come on. Let's get out of here before they start looking for her."

We climbed down and headed back to the car.

"Are we keeping it?" I asked, looking at the baby.

"Yes, you cold-hearted bastard," Tyra said. I shrugged and we got into the car.

"Where are we going?" he asked.

"Back to L'viv, to our mates. The Resistance. You didn't think we were out here all on our own, on some sort of romantic quest, did you? Are you hungry? We got any food left, Yuri?" I nodded towards the pack. Tyra talked as he tore into bread and cheese. "We call them ETs from the movie. That bloody Spielberg thing. Some people call them Messengers, but I think that just gives them too much bloody importance. They came five years ago. Dropped down out of the sky and nailed everybody they could get their hands on. 'Embraced,' they call it. By bloody golden monsters. My husband was embraced. I hope they all rot in hell."

"Aliens," he managed to say through a mouthful of bread. "An alien invasion."

"That's right."

"Is that why Russia dropped out of the war?"

"Yep."

"Where did they come from?"

"How the hell should I know?"

"What do they want?"

"Us. You. Everyone."

"What for?"

Tyra shrugged. "Who knows? Look, if something wants to eat you alive, do you ask why or do you run?"

"Neither," he said. "You kill it."

"Ah. We just haven't figured out how. Until you came along with that lovely corrosive stuff. We have got to find a way to churn that stuff out by the bloody barrel."

You would think that Mr. Thompson would have had many questions—

after all, how often is there an alien invasion? But no, once he'd eaten, all he wanted to do was tell his own war story. Typical.

"So there I was, in the ruins of Rzeszów—"

"Poland's still there?" I asked, surprised.

"Barely," he said.

"What about Przemýsi?"

"Gone." Tyra elbowed me in the ribs, and I shut up. Let him talk. "I was mopping up pockets of resistance. Most of my squadron had been killed in a surprise counter-attack and the rest of us had gotten scattered. My neurotransmitter locked in on an enemy stronghold..."

A long story, full of the usual twists, turns, hair-raising escapes, endless violence. I believed most of it: I'd heard worse. I'd done worse. I soon tuned him out, and thought about Przemýsi being gone... But why shouldn't it be gone? Six years of war, what a waste...

He talked, I drove, over the last scrubby hill and down into the lush meadows on the other side. Spring again, the meadows full of wildflowers and birds. I heard a gasp: in the rearview mirror, Mr. Thompson's face shook with a longing so desperate it could have passed for grief.

I felt sorry for him, so I stopped the car. He went and waded in the knee-deep grass. When he came back, he was holding a buttercup.

Tyra and I were leaning against the car, smoking cigarettes. "Ready?" she asked.

"No sterilants," he croaked.

"Yes."

"It's beautiful." He whispered that.

"Yes."

"You have no idea..."

"There's a price," Tyra said, bless her bitter little heart.

We got home at night. The ETs were everywhere, of course. The golden planes of light, their engravings writhing like snakes, lit up the sky, throbbing around and through almost every human being we saw.

"How many people have they taken?" he asked.

"Too damn many," Tyra replied.

"What's made you immune?"

"We hate Them," Tyra answered.

"Speak for yourself," I said. "I don't give a damn one way or the other."

"All right, so I hate Them. They don't like to be hated. Wouldn't think They were suckers for popularity, would you?"

I pulled up next to an old building and stopped the car. "Here we are. Don't worry. Here They don't come."

That night we watched him glut on meat and vegetables and bread, get spinning drunk on vodka. You could tell he felt like hell the next morning, but he kept everything down and lumbered up to breakfast with the stubborn determination of the starving.

"Yuri, come, see the new pamphlets," Lena said, the silly little bitch.

"Oh, God," Tyra groaned. "A new bunch of crap."

"What are they?" Mr. Thompson asked.

"Propaganda," I said. "Saying the ETs are on a mission from God."

He laughed, but then shook his head. "It's what they all say, God help us." I laughed at that.

"But what if it's true?" Lena asked.

"Oh, bloody wonderful," Tyra snarled. "Now you're starting to waver."

"No," Lena said. "No, no, no." But she was, of course. She was the type. Soon, I thought, I would have to arrange something. Scare her away or hand her over… Meantime, the baby would keep her occupied for a while.

"Gleb here is going to break down the components in that corrosive you brought," Tyra said. "And then we'll manufacture as much as we can."

"You better be careful with that stuff," Mr. Thompson replied. "It's been known to explode."

"I am a chemist," Gleb said. "I know what I'm doing."

And he did. I gave Mr. Thompson a quick tour of the place, gratified to see how surprised he was at what we had.

"My God, you could do anything here," he said, looking around. "I don't understand. How are you getting away with this? Why haven't They shut you down?"

"They don't care," I replied. "They have so many people that we are irrelevant. It is very insulting."

Mr. Thompson was useless in the lab, knowing nothing and not very good at learning. He was of the energetic type, always moving. So he came foraging with the rest of us, and in that he had talent. For the next couple of days we were all busy, getting the supplies for Gleb and Denis.

Then it was time for them to work and the rest of us to rest. We had a little dinner party—when Mr. Thompson was not moving, he liked to be eating—with songs and vodka as everyone told their story.

"They came five years ago. They came down out of the sky all over Russia…"

"It was all so fast. One night, none, the next night, everywhere! I stood out in the square and watched Them come down. I thought They were beautiful, like golden clouds…"

"'Of hammered gold and gold enameling,'" I quoted, under my breath.

"Bloody fool." Tyra has little appreciation for poetry.

"Moscow was saturated with Them. The next day, the President resigned. Obshchy—"

"No, it was Volochek!"

"Let me finish! Volochek was President. But Obshchy was Foreign Minister, and he pulled us out of the war. That I didn't mind."

"So, have you all been approached by one?"

The "Nos" resounded. I almost laughed. You could feel the humiliating suspicion that the ETs hadn't really tried…and no idea why…

Lena, flushed with vodka, was looking at Mr. Thompson with a desire that did not suit her childlike face. "Tell him your story, Lena," I whispered. "It will interest him." She blushed and shook her head. "Shall I? Lena here came home and found her parents being embraced. It was not pretty. They were a very respectable, older couple, I remember them well, but Lena found them writhing on the floor, their eyes rolled back in their sockets, gabbling from foam-flecked mouths, interpenetrated… naturally, little Lena ran screaming out of the house." I took Lena's hand and kissed it lightly. "She came to us, and has never left. So tell him yours," I said to Tyra, who was glaring at both of us. It's good to stir her pot once in a while. "Tell him about Misha."

"Misha." Tyra's eyes looked off into the distance. "My husband. I went home, and one of Them was with him. Riding him like he was a bloody horse. And his face…I started screaming, and he said…he called it…" She wiped her eyes. "And he had the gall to tell me…that one of Them would come for me…we could all be happy together. I wanted to kill him. I think I tried, I don't remember. I bolted. When I went back he was gone. He's been gone ever since. Oh, he's still alive. But he's gone. He's bloody gone from me. Oh, God, I can't stand it." She threw her glass across the room and it sprayed against the wall in wet shards.

"Come, Tyra," I said, taking her arm. I knew what she needed. What she wanted. "Let's go."

We walked to the small café not far from our headquarters and stood in a doorway across the street. I smoked while Tyra watched her husband as he worked, as he moved, as he breathed. I find Misha small and dark and uninteresting. I have often thought how ridiculous it is, that gracile gold magnificence rising through little Mikhail Andropov as he sweeps the floor. Almost as ridiculous as when he brought home his magnificent Australian wife, now trembling at my side. But there is nothing ridiculous—except its object—in Tyra's desire. Today he looked up, saw Tyra, and waved. Smiling. Tyra groaned, somewhere between heartbreak and passion, and I took her home to let the waves of it break over me.

Then we slept. I woke first, and tucked her in nicely before I left the bedroom. It's the little touches that count. Then I went into the main room and put the samovar on.

"How's Tyra?" Mr. Thompson asked.

"She's fine." I sat down and lit a cigarette. "I took her to see Misha. Her husband."

"He's still around?"

"Where should he be? It upsets her, but she cannot stop herself. She loves him, she wants him, she needs him… Luckily, I am here, and I know how to handle her. Tea?"

"Yes, please. I went for a walk this morning."

"Did you?"

"Yes. It's…it's overwhelming. I went to the park. Down by the river. There are roses there…beds and beds of roses… I'd forgotten what they smelled like. And the water, that sound…"

"I have a book of Wordsworth, if you'd like to borrow it."

"Don't make fun of me."

"I wouldn't dream—"

"You've never seen a sterilant cloud turn Brittany into grey mud. England's nothing but dust and rubble. I've seen bombs, biochem agents, sterilant clouds. Did you know about Influenza H-V? Half the world died in a month! The whole world, everything outside, is burnt dust! And I sat there, in that park, with the sun warm on my face, and the smell of roses and sweet grass." His face was bleak for a man who had just experienced an overwhelming joy.

"Have some tea. Have you had any breakfast?"

"I ate before I went."

"Good. You must eat to live."

"I came back and started reading the pamphlets." He picked up one. "'The Second Secret of Fatima fulfilled. Russia will be converted and peace will be granted to the world.'"

"The usual propaganda."

"What if it's true?"

I said nothing.

"Well? Well?"

I sighed. I'd known this was coming from the time he'd come wading back through the meadow. "So what if it is? Sit down. Calm yourself. What I say to you, I say quite seriously. Say it is true. Say it is the finger of God. Go. Be embraced. Live in bliss, like Fyodor and Volya and Pavel and all the others."

"Why haven't you?"

"Alas, I am an atheist."

He looked at me for a while. "No, you're not. You're something else. You believe it's true, but…you've chosen against it."

"I have other interests."

"Tyra. Who's obsessed with her husband, who doesn't want her, and so she's with you. My God, I don't know which one of you is the sickest."

I shrugged. "You have spent the last six years burning everything you love to dust. I have Tyra and all I need—"

"But if this is from God—"

"There is no proof of that."

"What if there was? Proof?"

"Bring some."

He got up and walked out. I finished my tea, and went back to Tyra.

He returned two days later. I saw him come in the front door, and drifted back to the kitchen, from where I could watch and interfere quickly if necessary. Tyra looked up from the book she was reading and asked, sharply, "What is it?"

He stood there for a minute, his face irradiated, his eyes glazed. Gold planed around him. "I came back to tell you the truth. You're all wrong about the ETs. The pamphlets are telling the truth. Your husband is trying to save you, to bring you—"

A bullet tore through his chest. Lying on the ground, he looked up at Tyra, who put her gun to his temple. "But it's true!" he whispered.

"I don't care," she hissed, and killed him.

I came running in. "Tyra! What have you done?"

She looked at me, her face hard. "He said…he said…" And then she burst into hysterical sobs.

I took the gun away from her and took her in my arms. "There, there. My Tasha. It's all right. I'll take care of everything. He didn't understand. Tasha. It's all right."

I calmed her with vodka and caresses and tucked her into bed. Then I took Mr. Thompson's body down to the river. An ET arced in hammered gold beside me, perhaps his.

"Leave me alone," I said to it, as I rolled Mr. Thompson into the river. "I have all I want without you."

Then I went back inside, to hold Tyra against the night.

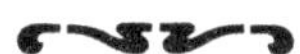

98% Graves

Adam Sass

Eleanor Graves received Last Rites for the ninth time since her decline into death began last year. "So furious this isn't the end," she told her three best friends after it became clear she was to go on living. The eighty-year-old heiress rolled her eyes, and pink diamonds jingled on silver bracelets as she chugged the remaining Veuve Clicquot without stopping for breath. "I hate this brand"—her hearty Norwegian accent uplifted an otherwise toneless voice—"Why does everyone make such a fuss?"

"It's not the real champagne," Carol said—sun-browned, wrapped in scarves, and hiding behind mammoth sunglasses. "Darling, it's someone's approximation of it, darling. You couldn't afford a shooter of the real thing. You can scarcely afford to be Eleanor."

"That is a terrible, *terrible* excuse for bad booze." She fiddled with the long opal she wore on her forefinger and sneered at the rapidly populating nightclub, an Old Hollywood thing with brick-red Persian tapestries draping walls the color of honey. They always selected this club because of its evergreen charm—it cheered Eleanor up through breakups, through the loss of a cat, through a mugging—but today, it dragged on her. Eleanor hadn't died yet, and everything became an irritant.

The old woman's younger friends agreed beforehand to humor her shitty attitude for at least a little bit, but the nightclub was filling up with dozens of American soldiers. Those privates wouldn't bang themselves.

Marcie suckled the last vodka drops off her dirty martini's olive. The youngest of the four, Marcie wasted her glamour with such bad manners. Her world-famous curves, withered by cocaine; her gospel voice, drunk down the toilet; by 27, Marcie was dead. She'd been dead five years, longer than any of them—except for Eleanor, of course, her body refusing to expire.

The starlet scanned the bar below for her pick of the soldiers. Her eyes moved past Vietnam ones and Iraq ones—all crew cuts. She declared earlier she wanted a D-Day officer boy; she wanted hair, floppy blond hair or pomaded black hair, didn't matter.

"This one." Eleanor clicked her tongue at Marcie as the girl finally devoured the olive. "Drink-hungry and man-hungry and completely ignoring me."

"I worked a long goddamn day," Marcie said, staggering up from their private table, "and I ain't spending another session listening to you wail."

"Ah, this is a one-way street, then? We hear you out when you're blue, but you don't have to reciprocate." Eleanor looked for understanding from November, but the former beauty queen was busy adjusting her pink satin bustline; implanted double-Ds constantly threatened to boil over the top. She was purposely evading this confrontation. Eleanor sighed. "Go. Grab a man."

Marcie swirled a tipsy hand over the old woman's sunken cheek; she kissed her forehead and continued down foot-lit steps to her soldiers. She snatched two by their collars—a lithe Italian and a husky, All-American blond—and led them willingly across the dance floor. The trio vanished into a parlor behind velour curtains.

"You used to be fun," Carol said, stony behind her sunglasses. "Don't blame Marcie. You chose to be Eleanor."

Eleanor despised this plain data-speak about the program. Immersion was the entire point. There were risks of picking Eleanor from the lineup; the heiress's presence in the nightclub was a glitch—she had been entered prematurely when she sunk into a coma and had not been properly erased when she emerged. "I am Eleanor," she said, sliding a cigarette from a sapphire case.

"Darling, please choose someone else." Carol massaged her scalp through a headscarf. "They'll delete her if she doesn't die soon."

Beyond the parlor curtains, two soldiers hollered and Marcie hit her fabled upper register.

The soldier wouldn't have to be careful with Eleanor's aged body—she had all the strength and endurance of her operator. Black and tall with razor cheekbones, the Vietnam soldier gripped Eleanor's legs under her peach lace dress and devoured her neck with a beast's energy. She let herself be serviced in their private lovers' parlor. Miles away, her operator felt the pleasure.

"Oh," Eleanor giggled and stopped the soldier's hands moving any further up her hosed thigh. "You don't have to do that." The man stood still and awaited further instructions. "Um…how are you?"

"I'm sorry," the soldier said. "I'm a program."

Eleanor groaned and sloshed back gin from her garter flask. "I know *that*. I'm feeling a lot of anxiety."

"Let me try something." The soldier unfastened his jungle green fatigues and presented a thick, heaving chest. Eleanor stared and took another sip. The soldier moved closer. "Did this solve your problem?"

Eleanor waved her flask to ward him off: "Maybe I should just watch for a little bit." The soldier dropped his fatigues to his bare ass and ran mammoth hands up and down his lovingly detailed backside. Eleanor's attention fell on his dimpled lower back, and her hard lips relaxed.

"I'm sorry I'm not better at this," Eleanor said to the back of her stripping soldier. "It's not fair. I don't feel the least bit grand, even though I'm paying out my eyeballs for Eleanor Graves—"

The soldier's neck exploded.

She shrieked, and his head craned backwards like he was staring at the sun. It kept craning until the mechanical slit in his throat opened entirely. Eleanor clasped jeweled fingers over her eyes as her lover's head hung, mostly severed, off the back of his neck. Lifeless, upside-down eyes met Eleanor's.

A hundred imperceptible gears spun, filling her ears with poorly oiled squeaks. A pedestal emerged from the hole in the soldier's neck, bearing a phone, its edges lit up in icy blue.

"Sir?" Eleanor asked, stepping closer.

"*Eleanor Graves?*" asked a woman's digitized voice from the phone.

"Shit." Eleanor finished the flask.

"*You are in violation of the Life Copyright of Eleanor Caroline Graves. Terminate your identity immediately, or you will be indebted to the Countess Graves in the amount of 7.3 million dollars, or until such time—*" Her flask shattered on the parlor tile in a billion silver pixels.

"Sonofabitchwhore!" Eleanor screamed as she drop-kicked the severed head of her paramour into the nightclub. A woman in white, her hair stringy from heroin chic, yelped as the head soared over the other patrons and struck her chest. She detonated into a trillion pixels. Thirty

American soldiers and their lusty intendeds turned as one to see Eleanor hunched, arms out like a feral cat, over her soldier's headless body.

"Baby, what's all this goddamn noise?" Marcie asked, emerging from the parlor behind Eleanor and climbing back into her little black dress. Her two American Johnnies stepped ahead of her and advanced on Eleanor. Their necks opened.

"*You are in violation of the Life Copyright*—" they said in unison.

"Kissmyassmotherfuckers!" Eleanor snatched a brass chair and swung it like a baseball bat at Marcie's soldier boys. They swooped and evaded her wild beat-down. "Gityoufuckers!"

Crunch. The burly, blond soldier took the brass square in his gut. The Italian soldier lunged at Eleanor, but her beauty queen friend reached her first.

"Stop flippin' out," November said in a druggy haze as she dragged the old woman screaming from the dance floor. Eleanor scratched at November's arms. "Ow. Ow. Quit."

Marcie scooped Eleanor's legs, and they carried her up curved marble stairs to their veranda table. "Killthosepricksshateyou!" The bar soldiers looked up at the women and opened their necks.

"What *has* happened?" Carol asked, waiting for her friends in a lounging, Hollywood repose.

"Apparently, we have to leave," Marcie said, lowering Eleanor—writhing—to the floor.

"She attacked those programs," November said, massaging her cut-up arms.

Carol rage-gasped at Eleanor but still did not remove her sunglasses. "My horoscope said you would do something like this!"

"Best I go home," Marcie said. "I got an early meeting."

November swallowed two ruby pills from her purse and said, "Bye all. I had fun time traveling with you."

"No, darling," Carol said, "reality simulation, not time travel."

"'kay."

Eleanor clawed herself to her feet, clanging heavy necklaces as she did. "The bitch is suing me! Seven million. They're not taking her away—"

Crack—crack—crack! One by one, the soldiers turned on their suitors, vaporizing rocker chicks and lipsticked movie stars just by touching them. Pixels snow-globed in the club until the four friends were the only users left. Carol smacked Eleanor's white up-do. "Now everyone

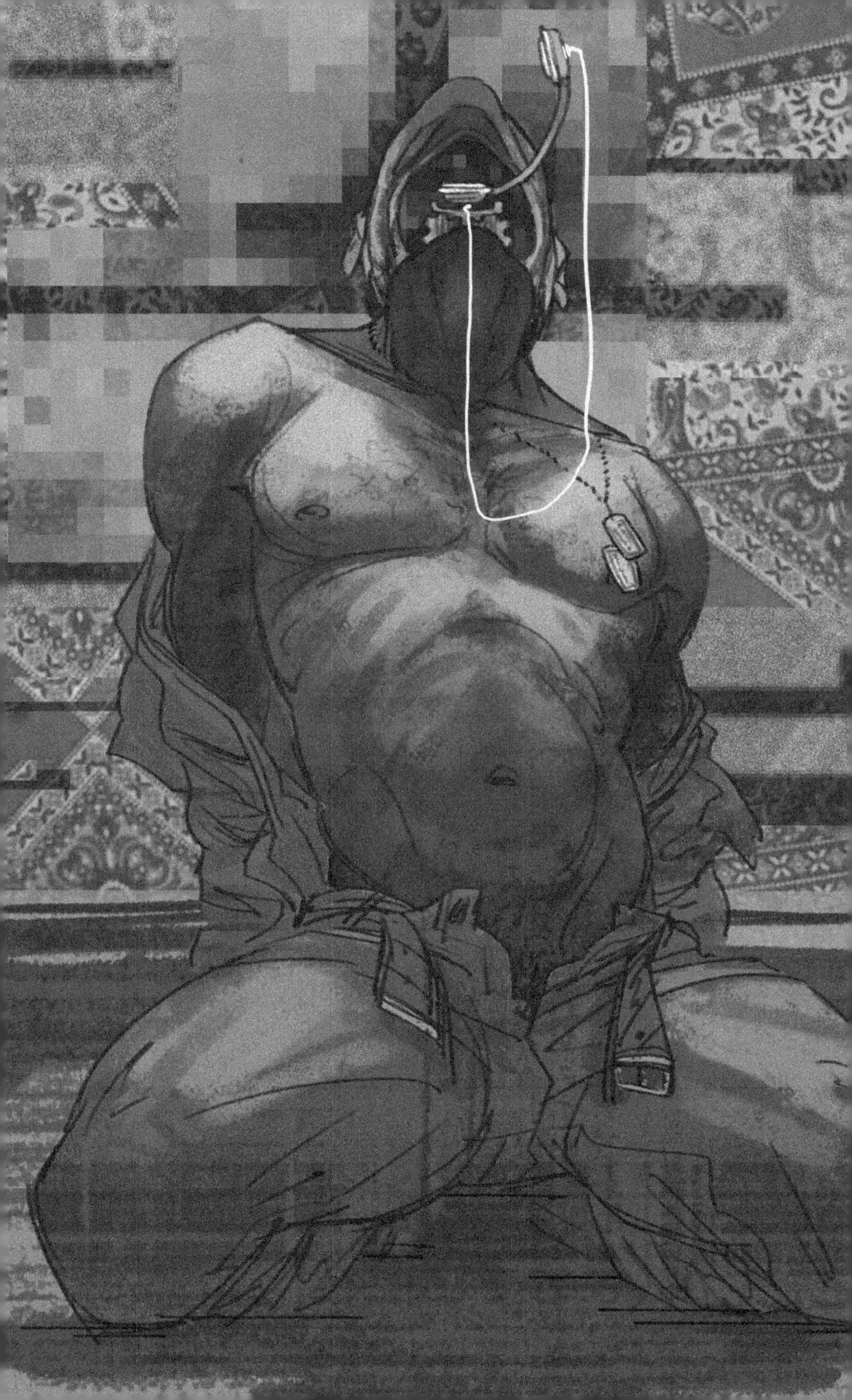

has to go home."

"She was supposed to die last night, and this wouldn't be a problem."

"You should have given up Eleanor when I told—"

"*Eleanor Graves, terminate your identity immediately,*" shouted the phones in every soldier's neck. "*Carol Klipner, November Grace, Marcie Rose, for abetting this violation, you will each terminate your identities as well.*"

"Aw, fuck *you*," Marcie growled at Eleanor, the heiress unable to stop her bloodshot eyes from bugging. "You got any idea how early I had to get here to reserve Marcie?"

"You're not taking Eleanor," she cried at the battalion. "She's fabulous, and she belongs to all of us! SSSSUCK MY DICK!"

Pop. A company officer fired his rifle. Marcie and Eleanor dove to the carpet, but the officer had hit his target: Carol projectile vomited a shower of silver pixels. Her sunglasses evaporated bit by bit, and she was gone. *Pop.* November launched backwards in a horizontal waterfall of pixels.

Marcie pulled her long diva's legs up to her chest and stayed hidden behind the veranda railing. Eleanor clutched the floor, muttering, "I wanted her and no one else did. She had money, and she didn't give a damn about anything."

"I'm feeling you," Marcie said, "but, girl, it's time to let this lady go."

"I serve coffee to assholes in a business park, and I…and all I do all day is give a damn. I get to be her, and I still can't grab a man when he's stripped in front of me." Eleanor grunted as she rolled from her knees to her back. Dozens of boot steps marched in time up the marble towards them. "When is it my turn to be the out-of-control, psycho bitch?"

Marcie laughed full from her chest and climbed up on wobbly stilettos. "Shit, dumpling, you were the craziest, mouthiest disaster I ever saw tonight. You'd make Eleanor proud."

"Yeah?"

"I don't lie. Come on—" She held out a sinewy arm. Eleanor whined from the floor but grabbed her friend's hand anyway. The soldiers reached the veranda. Thirty sculpted men in uniforms of every stripe confronted Marcie and Eleanor. The women held up their arms in surrender.

The D-Day boy—neck already opened—approached: "*Eleanor Graves, you are in violation of the Life Copy—*"

"Just do it, trick," Marcie said. And then the officer battered the butt of his rifle across her head, spraying pixels over Eleanor.

Do you willingly terminate your identity as Eleanor Caroline Graves? Failing to cooperate willingly leaves you liable for damages up to and including 7.3 million dollars."

Eleanor shut her eyes, diamond earrings jingling as she nodded. "I am not Eleanor Graves. My name is Peter Stockton."

Peter woke staring at the neon-flashing jukebox that connected all twenty-four simulator chairs. House music seeped in from the go-go stage in the next room. The chairs were empty but for his. A wall mirror in front of him reflected the operator behind Eleanor: his mundane complexion, not Eleanor's imperious glares; his glasses, not Eleanor's crystal blue eyes; his young, doughy, brown face, not Eleanor's porcelain, aged glamour. She was gone.

"What's up?" asked the twinky boy in the doorway. The long-haired, white scarecrow held two vodka sodas and stood next to a torn poster: *Hot & Fabulous 4eva! UberDrag simulators Thurs Nights @ Casa Fuerte!*

"Hi," Peter said. "Did I clear the room?"

"You did indeed," said the boy. "Everyone's pretty mad. Brought you a drink so you could wait it out here."

"Oh." Peter took the vodka soda from the twink he'd barely spoken to in real life but shared endless debates with as Marcie. He sifted his pockets for dollar bills.

"My treat, stop."

"Thank you. So, what, I gotta leave out the back?"

"Naw, everyone's gonna get their partial refund, get a drink, get a dude, forget all about it. Come on—" Marcie's operator held out a sinewy arm. Peter looked away on instinct and took his friend's hand. They sipped and walked together to the flashing jukebox. Instead of songs, there were names of forty infamous women, from the faboo-but-damned Marcie Rose to the troublemaking, not-yet-dead Countess Graves. The twink jabbed a finger at Eleanor's name. "I knew you were a barista. I'd totally seen you before."

"Hope the lawyers don't find me. I don't make seven million dollars on nine an hour."

"If anything, the company's liable. You'll just get a little warning e-mail.

You'll be back in the saddle soon." Marcie's operator smiled at Peter—his smile was wide and pretty, front teeth overlapping slightly. Peter smiled back.

"If you gotta choose someone new, can I be Marcie next?"

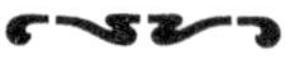

Drusten

Marcus S. Robin

Serena sat back and wiped away some tears, letting out the anguish that hadn't registered until she had heard Sean's voice. In the middle of an old road, out behind the corn and the rusted oil derricks, Serena cried for all of the greed in the universe, for Billy, and for herself.

She hit pause on the stream and stopped the rusty truck in the middle of the road. Leaning on the steering wheel, Serena pressed her eyes into the sleeves of an old flannel shirt she was wearing that once belonged to Billy, and let the tears soak into them. It had been 3 months since she got word from her colleagues about Drusten. They told her the sentinel vessels that were monitoring the pumping operations had finished compiling their reports, but for the details she wanted she would have to wait for Sean's communique. He had been the only survivor.

Serena first met Sean when Billy had him over to the farm for the Drusten launch party. They were practically spitting images of each other and one would never guess they weren't brothers. Dipping Copenhagen. Lifting weights. The Merchant Marines was their brotherhood. There was a difference Serena had noticed, though.

Sean and Billy were having a beer in the driveway, occasionally glancing at the stars. "Kepler M was a giant clusterfuck. But here's the ironic part, crystal operations are a walk in the park compared to oil. Those jarheads on Kepler M should have known better than to blow that geode cap with that much energy, but they had to show off to B Pump. Now their mommies and daddies are burying shreds of their baby boys instead of their whole stupid corpses," Sean said at the time. Serena had never heard Billy speak as bluntly as Sean about the folly of other marines. He just nodded in agreement.

"I'd rather come back in shreds than not come back home at all," said Billy, raising his can.

"Hoorah," said Sean, toasting with Billy.

Hoorah, Serena murmured into her sleeves. She had to laugh about it. Sean had been right about Kepler M at that party so many months ago.

Incredibly cocky marines make incredibly cocky mistakes. Billy wasn't one of those kinds of marines, and she didn't feel that Sean was one either.

Serena breathed deep, blew her nose into a sleeve, and pressed play on the stream.

"…You should have tried telling Marshall that an excursion at that time of day was a bad idea, Serena. Because when I tried, Marshall looked at me like I shit my pants and yelled at me to get the damn thing in order. I really made an effort and explained to him that the suits were only rated for 600 degrees. Questioning a superior officer while in orbit isn't exactly out of the ordinary, as you know. Mission designers can't plan for every pitfall and sometimes commanding officers don't know any better. Questions or no questions though, Marshall was going to make damn sure every last bit of that ichor we were sent to wrench out of Drusten was wrenched out on time. No one can say I didn't try to at least postpone the mission, even if I was being selfish and just trying to stay out of the heat.

"It was 450 degrees on the surface and climbing, and the radiation levels were registering off the damn scale. Marshall—in that Parris Island way I'm sure Billy's told you about—wasn't hearing any excuses, though. He personally inspected the suits, he told us, and if we insisted on being maggots about getting a little tan then maybe the excursion could be ramped up to a full recon. Hell, he'd been in worse conditions on Gratata, you see, with shoddier comfort suits and fewer men, the enemy at their heels, living to tell the tale… An inspiring story the first time I heard it.

"But you know Billy, Serena. He was the authority on petrobiotics and sedimentary basin geology, opinionated, the finest squad leader, but a total rollover when it came to being a marine. He would have eaten Marshall's shit up and asked for seconds if he were told it was compulsory to the mission.

"That hell on the surface was going to test our limits. The Golds on the *Murmansk* reported that the rigs on the far side of the landing zone were clear according to their preliminary scans, and the oiloids that had poked around curiously during the near side extractions the day before appeared to have had retreated sometime during the long night. They couldn't say for sure where they had gone, but in their limited experience the oiloids tended to avoid the high temperatures like anything sane

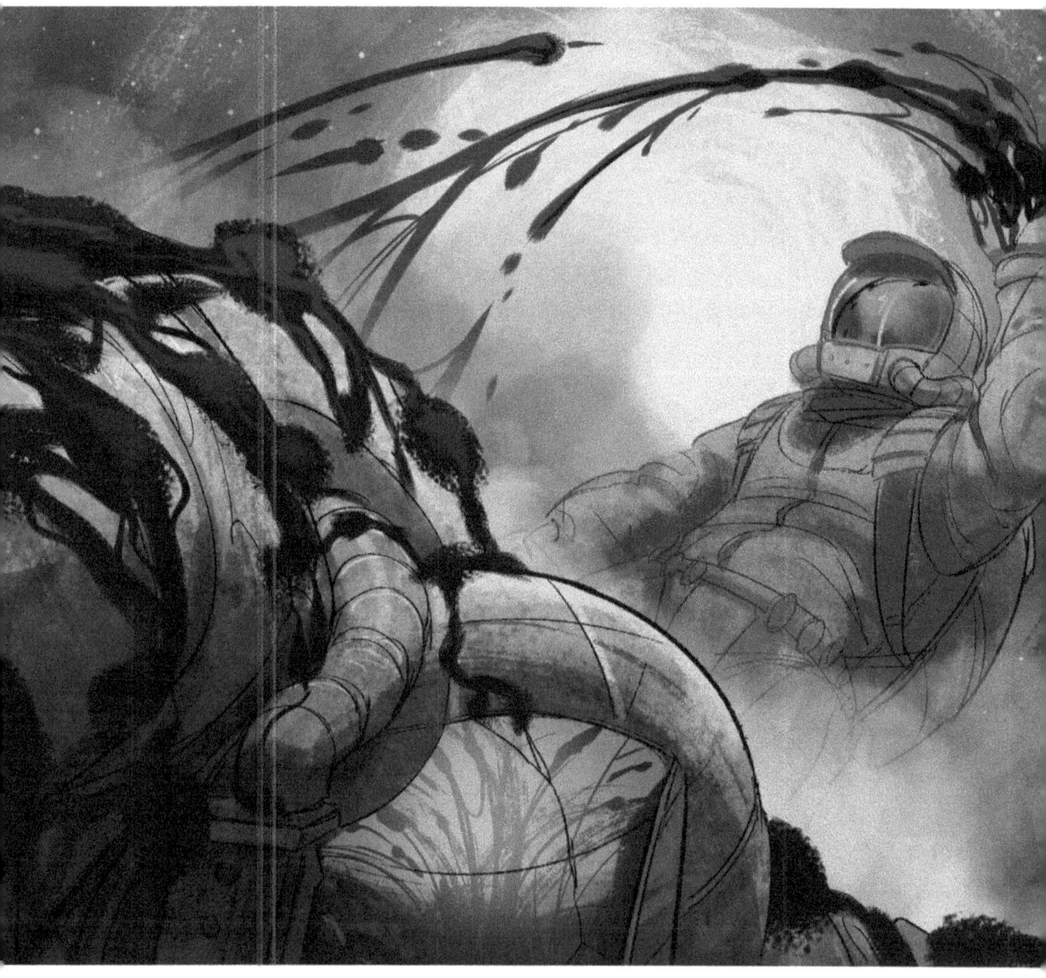

would. Most of the oil in the zone had been siphoned already, but rather than wait another 36 hours for dark, and for cooler temperatures, they wanted a day crew to pull the last tanker full and be done with it. Billy plotted our time line based on the Golds' readings, and reassured us that the suits would hold up perfectly fine. It was Marshall that ordered us, but it was Billy that motivated us."

This was exactly what Serena was talking about when she had told Billy to think again about accepting the mission. The Merchant Marine contract was from a venture that was new to outer planet prospecting. They had been successful within the Sol system, and soon they had success in one other, true enough, but they were still green compared to other ventures from which Billy had accepted contracts. In her experience, the proposal seemed exceedingly arrogant with plenty of references to their success in technology development for in-orbit gas extraction and refinement while prospecting Jupiter, but nothing about their margin of error, or the risks involved on Drusten.

"This seems off, Billy," Serena remembered saying. "They laid claim on a barely explored or understood planet, saw it was mostly just desert, and decided to blindly go in to prospect? The oil fleets that are most successful today are the ones that have been doing it the longest on Earth. It's just—"

"It's a test mission, honey. They want to see how quickly they can set up and get out. Besides, the payoff is huge. Shropa will pay a fortune. They're signing on the whole crew because they know our record and they know we can help them exceed their expectations," Billy interrupted. "Help them get an edge on competing prospectors and in developing their own legacy. We may even get signed on long term if the money's there."

The farm needed modernization. Serena couldn't argue with the figures the contract had proposed. So off Billy went, and back in the truck Sean's voice continued on like an armed forces radio drama.

"It was hard for us to not be as optimistic as Billy was while we were faced with certain danger, Serena. He said he was confident in us and our ability to carry out the plan. 'I'm going to make diamonds out of you coprolites one of these days,' he said to us in his best Marshall impersonation. 'But first let's do this.' That was Billy.

"Serena, I want you to understand something. The oiloid that trapped Billy, and eventually the wave of them that trapped us all, didn't know him. Hell, they didn't know they were even supposed to care. He fell over the side of a sloped cliff when the quakes caused the land to fault right near us, and I heard him struggling. I reached down, grabbed his hand and tried to free him from its pull, but the sun was relentless and the damn thing just boiled that much hotter; the quakes became that much more intense. While holding Billy's glove, and struggling to remove him from the growing puddle, I saw across the desert a geyser spring where there were no rigs. The oiloid column was taller than Burj Khalifa, and then there were others. Billy's grip left mine, and I ran.

"Billy deserved better than that. He deserved to grow old back home, driving that '57 Chevy pickup around those farm roads with you in the passenger seat. Going out for ice cream on a Sunday afternoon and then taking the long way home. His resting place should be there. Not under a sea of boiling oil creatures. I'm sorry I didn't die there with all of them."

Serena flippantly paused the stream again, growing impatient with Sean's curtness. "Jerk," said Serena to the stream player. The pickup's engine finally turned after she tried a few times to start it. She put it into gear and drove to some hills further up the road where there were some pecan trees planted.

She parked the truck under a tree on a hill overlooking the fields, and reached to the passenger seat, grabbing a file from her bag. Her colleagues had made available to her some of the reports from the sentinels. The reports went into great detail about the oiloids and how the entire species was one organism, having existed under the surface of Drusten's ancient sedimentary basins for ages until the Merchant Marines showed up. It also mentioned the sacrifice of the crew, but only quickly, and then proceeded to talk about the prospect of future operations on Drusten, and the endless sea of oil that now existed there. She threw the file back into the seat, letting the papers scatter everywhere.

Drusten sprang a leak and the bosses *of the cocky marines won. It only cost them Billy and a few others, but now everything's safe for orbital extraction. Hey, a new species never seen before that can regenerate itself over and over again? Fuck 'em. They'll pull that shit out faster than it can replicate, and drain the whole planet until the sun bakes the survivors, leaving it a husk. How did Earth ever survive us?*

Serena hit play on the stream and drove down the hill back to the road. There were calls to be made now, some things to shake up.

"Next time you have a drink, Serena, pour one for Marshall. He ordered us out there, and the suits were fine, but the poor bastard didn't know. No one knew what that shit was capable of in the godforsaken heat of that gravel pit planet. It wasn't going to be the heat that killed us, but no one knew that.

"Have one for the rest of the crew that didn't make it on Drusten, too Serena. And have one for me, in Billy's honor."

Serena punched the gas.

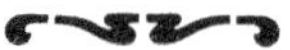

The Priestesses of Light

David W. Landrum

alayna Yonvi looked out at the audience and then over at Aaron. Through the windows, she could see the snow falling. The bad weather had not kept the protestors away. A good-sized crowd of angry, vociferous people were demonstrating against her appearance. She sighed, crossed her legs, and leaned over to Aaron. "Any news about the protest?"

"They're reporting the crowd at five thousand. There's a counter-rally too, close to the same size. You'd think that many people wouldn't come out in a snowstorm to protest the curing of a disease."

She shook her head at the irony. Twenty years ago, Lalayna and her medical team (including Aaron) had begun the vaccination program that eradicated juvenile blindness from the planet Suva. For centuries the wily virus that could disguise itself so effectively had eluded detection—until, one night, again by chance, she had isolated a sample. After that, finding a way to prevent its entry into the bodies of the children upon which it preyed had been a simple task. She wondered, as she sat on the platform and watched the room fill with dignitaries, if the protest would turn into a riot.

She could see them through the large windows of the meeting hall. A mass of people stood in the wintry mix, some of them carrying signs, all of them rhythmically raising clenched fists and chanting, though she could not hear the words of the chant.

The Chief Priestess would be there, she remembered, and this would perhaps have a moderating effect—or at least she hoped it would—on the anger of the traditionalists. Kind and gentle, the priestesses exemplified restraint and true religious piety. They displayed this even to her, who had diminished their ranks and brought about the present crisis and the unrest no one could have possibly anticipated when her team undertook the project.

Aaron leaned over. "I just heard the priestesses won't be here."

Lalayna felt a hollowness in her chest.

"Why not?"

"No explanation. Let's hope they got stuck in the snowstorm—and pray they're not siding with the traditionalists."

Lalayna did not reply. Her chagrin at the stupidity religion often engendered rose up. She let her right hand fall on the wooden arm of the chair she sat in and began to drum her fingers loudly—an old habit she fell into when vexed and frustrated. She and her medical team had cured a disease that had tormented the people of this world for millennia. Now factions within the planet's religious-political structure vilified her so much that the government had assigned guards to protect her quarters.

She shifted, once more thinking she should not have worn a short skirt. But she had worn it because Locran would be watching on TV.

At 42, she still could turn heads. Her body had remained trim and she had not put on weight. She was not at the age where her skin had begun to sag, though it would do that in a few years. Locran would think her beautiful when he saw her for the first time on their wedding night. She had not slept with him. Lalayna Yonvi had blushed with embarrassment when she told her fiancé she was a virgin.

From a conservative, traditional family, his daughter a married priestess of Robinna, Locran had been delighted at the news. Lalayna did not say her condition resulted merely from default. She had no qualms about premarital sex. Religion, ethics, and morality had nothing to do with her being still untouched in her fourth decade of life. Her career had kept her out of bed. She had simply been too busy to have a relationship.

She reflected on this as she watched the lecture hall fill up. Her parents sacrificed for her to go to medical school and she wanted repay their sacrifices with success. As an undergraduate, she studied for hours and, when men got cozy with her, gently moved away from them. She did not want to get pregnant and did not want to become so emotionally involved she would neglect her progress as a student. She graduated at the top of her class, went on to train in interspace medicine (during which time she isolated the virus), served six years as an army doctor, and established a practice in her native Mervogia. At age thirty, she began researching diseases in the Besrid sector of space and became an expert physician and immunologist, not only for her own people but for Barzalians, Omrites, and Terrans. She eventually settled on Ascania, another free Barzalian world, to practice as a full-time physician.

On Ascania, the epiphany came. One winter noon, eating lunch and watching the snow fall outside the window of her office, she realized she was forty years old, unmarried, still a virgin, and without a single romantic prospect on this world or any other. She remembered sitting there, a forkful of salad halfway between the plate and her mouth. She had felt as cold and fruitless as the snowy landscape beyond her office window.

She had resigned herself to a single life. She had not missed being married in the past, so why should she crave such a thing now? Still, the loneliness her busy career had camouflaged all these years fell on her with force, bending her spirit under its long, accumulated weight. Four months later, she met Locran, a widower with a grown daughter. Within a year they were engaged.

A buzz stirred through the room. Dignitaries from the Suvan government walked up on the platform. The ceremony would get underway now. The people stood for the Pledge, a short statement of dedication that preceded every official function of the planet's ruling party, whichever of the planet's five or six bickering factions might be ruling for this four-year term. She rose and listened to the chorus of voices. She was happy that she felt no pain from the hymenectomy three days ago. It was healing. She would be in good shape for the wedding and for her first sexual experience.

Asha had noticed the thickened tissue when she came in for a gynecological examination.

"I'm not sure you'll have any problems, but"—she paused.

"But an old maid like me might not want to take the risk of something going wrong—especially after waiting this long to get laid?" Lalayna smiled.

"Well, I wouldn't put it that way," her friend returned, "but you don't want to take any chances. It would just be safer and surer if you had a hymenectomy. I can do it right now if you want."

Lalayna agreed. Two nurses came in and prepped her. Asha set up a viewing screen so Lalayna could watch the procedure.

"I do four or five of these a month," she said. "The women in this area of the planet are more predisposed to the condition."

Asha was an Omrite—one of that odd race of beings with light pink skin, green hair, and golden eyes and fingernails. She came to Suva as part of an interplanetary medical team and ended up settling on the planet. Omrite women who went into medicine or midwifery had to take vows of celibacy. A few months on Suva, though, made her abandon her chastity. She had never married, enjoyed a freewheeling lifestyle, and never lacked for men taken with her delicate beauty and exotic coloration. A capable physician, she had established a successful, profitable practice on Suva. She and Lalayna had been friends for years.

Asha's nurses put Lalayna in dorsal position, retracted her labia, and sprayed anesthetic. Masked and with gloves, her friend used forceps and small scissors, stretching tissue over the opening of her vagina and making incisions, the nurses periodically irrigating the area with saline solution. Lalayna watched on the screen. When Asha finished with the incisions, Lalayna said her vagina looked like a sea anemone. Asha laughed. She sutured the tags of flesh. This took a little longer, but she worked rapidly and efficiently. Lalayna had always thought Asha's small hands made surgery easy for her. She finished, evaluated, and removed the clamps. Lalayna sat up.

"Went fine. You'll be all set for your wedding night."

She smiled and gave her friend a small hug.

"Have you ever done this procedure?"

"Once or twice, I think."

"Well, I'm sure you know the precautions. No running marathons or jumping up and down. You should heal in a couple of days. I used dissolving sutures. You'll know if you're having problems."

Lalayna got dressed. She and Asha had lunch after this, during which she heard a long, interesting narrative her friend's romantic and sexual adventures over the past year.

Her mind returned to the ceremony. A Suvan official was making a long speech. Lalayna had felt a slight ache from the procedure the first day, but by the second day it was gone. Asha was a good surgeon.

The Suvan official finished. Polite applause filled the room. The woman coordinating the event stepped up to introduce Lalayna. She felt the slight nervousness she always felt before speeches, though she had given many. The priestesses were still not there, she noticed. The audience welcomed her warmly.

"Twenty years ago," she said, "I signed on to a medical team that came to the planet to investigate a parasite that caused widespread infantile blindness. I was only twenty-two years old, an intern still in medical

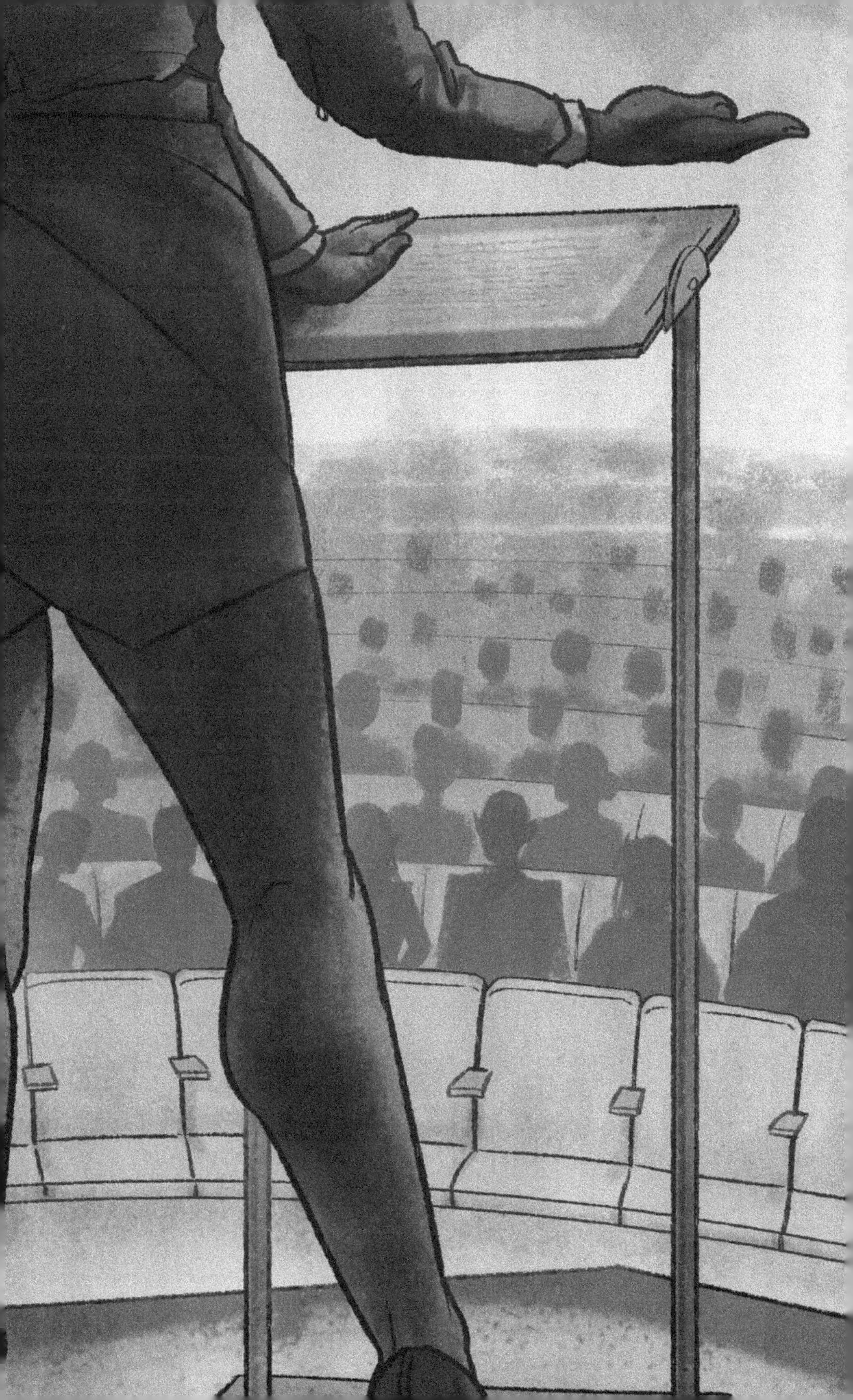

school. The parasite, *caecus vermis*, had the ability to break itself down, hide in the host body's DNA, making itself indistinguishable from the cells of the humanoid organism it had penetrated. One night, caring for a child who had the virus, and also a severe abrasion on his left upper arm from an automobile accident, I noticed a small organism wriggling on the surface of the abrasion. Thinking a blowfly or some other creature that lays its eggs in open wounds had gotten on this young boy, I snatched the thing away and sealed it in a sterile container. Subsequent tests revealed that this was, in fact, the parasite itself in its resting form.

"We discovered that the parasites are particularly vulnerable to rays of a certain frequency emitted by the light of Quanav, your moon, at certain phases and when its conjunction with the light of the Besrid nebula is maximal. These rays interfere with the sensory mechanisms the parasite has developed, and this enabled me to snag one with a pair of tweezers.

"After we captured a sample, it was easy to find a way to destroy *caecus vermis* and to vaccinate against it. In only a few months, infantile blindness due to the incursion of *caecus vermis* had been eradicated from planet Suva."

A few people applauded. Soon the entire room rumbled into applause. After a moment, the people stood.

"Thank you so much," Lalayna said when they had finished and sat down. "The elimination of infantile blindness has been a marvelous thing. I know that it has caused some religious debate on the planet—let us be frank and not avoid speaking of the obvious tensions with which we are dealing. The demonstration outside is, I'm certain, a reflection of the heartfelt concerns of many. I hope that the debate over this issue will be civil and will be conducted in a respectful and magnanimous fashion. I also hope that the Suvan government will continue to fund the Interplanetary Medical Endeavor which has saved thousands of children from blindness and brought so many other benefits to the medical and healthcare establishment of this world. Thank you all so much."

She sat down. Applause once more filled the room. But even as she reflected on her words, she saw the protesters outside. She thought of how religion could be an exasperating complication to medical advancement.

The people of Suva worshipped Robinna, but their priestesses had consisted entirely of women who were blind from *caecus vermis*. They would begin their training as children and live their entire lives in the temple complex that was the planet's central place of worship.

With the end of infantile blindness, religious contention began. Traditionalists said the Suvan priestesses must be blind and blocked the entrance of sighted girls into the convents. They campaigned to block some female children from vaccination against *caecus vermis* so they would be available as priestesses—a thing that appalled more liberal-minded Suvans. For twenty years the controversy raged. No new priestesses were ordained. The older ones began to die off and soon, especially in the provinces where religious sentiment was strong, the people felt the shortage of clergy.

The ruling party took steps to correct the situation and priestess who could see were admitted to the orders. *All this effort, talk, and trouble,* Lalayna thought, *over something as innocuous as a question of who could serve as a priestess.*

She heard the sound of shattering glass.

She gaped as the tall glass windows in the lecture hall shattered and collapsed in a cascade of glass shards. A rush of cold air and snow blew in and, following, flashes of blaster fire. She dove to the floor. Aaron cried out and fell, his upper body glowing from a hit. She tried to crawl over to help him, but by now the scene around her was mayhem. Blue and yellow streaks of energy filled the room as the police and soldiers exchanged shots with whoever had invaded the room. A cacophony of screams, curses, shouting, cries of pain, rang through the dome-shaped building. She had inched her way near Aaron when a soldier approached her.

"Back," he said. "Behind the curtain. There's a secure chamber."

Lalayna and a few other people crawled under the thick curtain behind the lectern, got up, and ran toward an open door. They entered a dark, quiet room.

She felt hands seize her, drag her to a chair, and bind her with rope. She struggled, but in moments they had secured her so she could not move. She looked about frantically, unable to see.

Someone lit a candle. Other candles appeared around her. A man walked forward in the dim, yellow light. He held a blaster pistol in one hand and what looked like an iron rod in the other. She realized the call to retreat to the room had been a set-up.

"Lalayna, from Mervogia" he said, smiling slightly. "It's an honor to meet you."

Too terrified to speak, or even to struggle, she stared back at him.

"Your speech was impressive. Don't you have anything to say now?"

"Who are you?"

He did not answer but pointed the blaster pistol at the iron rod in his hand. Its power beam contacted the end of the rod. In a moment, it glowed white-hot.

"I can't stop what you've set in motion, but I can ordain you as a priestess. We called them the Priestesses of Light because though they lived in darkness they gave light."

She screamed as he lowered the poker. It would be the last thing she saw, she thought, waves of cold fear running through her body when a voice rang out in the dark. She also realized—the irony was bitter—that if he blinded her she would be qualified to be one of the ancient priestesses in every aspect.

"Stop this at once."

The voice was female—it sounded like the voice of an older woman, though its authority made it clear and firm.

The man stood there, staring past Lalayna.

"Put the poker away. This moment."

As Lalayna watched, he handed the glowing iron poker to one of the other men holding candles. Lalayna felt a hand touch her shoulder.

"Are you all right, child?" the voice asked.

She saw an elderly woman she recognized.

"Lucine?" she asked.

"I hope you have not been harmed."

"No." She could hardly speak. "Thank you."

"I have only done what any decent woman would do. I'm sorry."

By now the room had filled. The Chief Priestess, Lucine, stood beside her. Soldiers and police rushed in. The lights came on. The man who had intended to blind her and those with him surrendered without a fight. The authorities bound them and took them away.

"You knew about this." She looked over at Lucine. "That was why you weren't present for the ceremony."

"We were back here all the while. We knew what Kennix intended to do and took steps to interdict his plan."

Lalayna trembled. A wave of nausea passed over her. She saw someone help Aaron across the stage. He was walking and conscious. He could not have been hurt too badly. She noticed, too, several other blind priestesses in the room. Lucine squeezed her shoulder.

"The goddess has protected you," she said.

Lalayna began to cry.

By now the room was flooded with police and soldiers loyal to the government. They untied her. Through the chaos, she saw Asha rush toward her. She had her medical bag. She touched Lalayna on the cheek and thigh—a gesture of intimacy among Omrite women.

"Did they harm you?"

She shook her head, sobbing. "They were going to blind me."

A look of disgust crossed Asha's face. Normally mild, cheerful, and pleasant, she looked like a different person when negative emotions possessed her.

"Let me look at your wrists. Do you feel any vaginal bleeding? Your sutures didn't break, did they?"

Lalayna did not feel blood. Her wrists were chaffed, but not badly. Asha bathed her face with a cool cloth. The lecture hall had quieted now. Cool air billowed through the broken windows and into the small room where she sat. She wanted to get her phone out and call Locran. He would hear about it on broadcast and fear for her. She needed to tell him she was all right.

Outside, the snow billowed, cloaking the earth with purity.

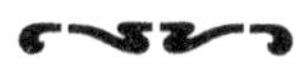

Crow Magnum Xix

Daniel Gooding

The last flashing light on the console blinks out, and Wallace Rushford-Sale is left in almost total darkness. The stacked video screens already conked out sometime mid-century, and now there is only black, with the white dust of stars scattered across his vision like lint on a seat cushion. Wallace Rushford-Sale himself is caked and waxy in appearance, and despite having been sealed in an airtight container for what could be hundreds of years, he too looks as though he has just been pulled from within the crease of this giant, cosmic sofa.

Clearly Wallace Rushford-Sale did not think this whole thing through. He does not now think this to himself however, as Wallace Rushford-Sale no longer thinks anything, having no cognitive thought and arguably no brain activity whatsoever; but his lack of foresight is obvious to anyone watching him. Not that anyone can see him anymore or even remember who he was, or that he was ever here in the first place. There is no memorial to Wallace Rushford-Sale back on Earth. There had been plans for some sort of edifice, commissioned, funded and largely designed by one Wallace Rushford-Sale, but at the end of the day it had come down to a choice, financially speaking, between a grotesque, building-sized effigy in central Detroit, Michigan and the Grumbletron9000; the latter had quickly won out.

The Grumbletron9000 was not the official brand-name of the machine, but had been thus named by the workmen who installed it in the window bank of the capsule. It is certainly just as well that Wallace Rushford-Sale was not in the room when they came up with this name; obviously he *was* physically in the room, in actual fact lying stiffly supine between the legs of the burly blue jumpsuit who screwed in the monitor, but fortunately he did not hear what was being said. The only thing registered by Wallace Rushford-Sale at that time was the upside-down ravine of the thick fabric's crotch, the occasional switch of light from the twisting screwdriver, and the intermittent grey snowflake drifting down towards his face, until another different colour suit entered his vision and, oblivious to his own hearing, instructed the blue jumpsuit to stop smoking on the job, and to show some goddamned respect for chrissake.

It is difficult to pinpoint the exact date of Wallace Rushford-Sale's death, largely due to the fact that it can be argued that he is still in some sense alive, and in equal measure because it is hard to say whether he ever really died at all. His being embalmed would suggest some measure of fatality, as would his continued residence in a perpetual vacuum, floating in another much wider vacuum. Lack of pretty much all bodily functions is another strong indicator of deceasement. But while Wallace Rushford-Sale may be lacking in such things, as well as emotion, thought, speech, movement and sensory reception, he still somehow is able to register colour and movement. To what extent he really registers these is also unclear, but if you were to place a newspaper or magazine in front of him, the words and pictures would show up in his vision as they would in the viewfinder of a camera. There just isn't a button he can press to store these images to memory.

Countless scientists and NASA technicians had explained this to Wallace Rushford-Sale over and over again, that this was the only possible way to keep him "alive," so to speak, for anywhere near this long: that although he would be able to see out of the window the whole time, as well as the inside of the capsule, without the interruption of blinking or sleep, there would be no guarantee of any emotional response or definitive recognition on his part, assuming of course that the cell battery implant in his brain didn't malfunction at any time. But Wallace Rushford-Sale said that this was all fine. Besides which, as he would often say with a prophetic placing of the hand on the arm of whomever he happened to be addressing, you never knew, did you?

The important thing, as far as Wallace Rushford-Sale was concerned, was that he would be going further into space than anyone either living or dead had ever gone, or possibly ever would go; and while he may not be able to react or interact with whatever he may or may not see out there, the fact would remain, though alone with him in the capsule, that he had seen these things and others had not. Whatever might drift across his empty vision would not be encountering another similar pair of eyes for possibly hundreds or thousands of years.

How Wallace Rushford-Sale had made his millions back on Earth is now unknown to him, or indeed anyone else: winning rollover lottery ticket, earth-shattering legal claims payout, substantial family inheritance, eccentric industry tycoon (though anyone who knew him personally, were they still alive, would laugh off suggestions of his being some kind of financial or business guru). Whatever his origins, his immediate circumstances came down solely to this cold, still reflection doubled in the two dead screens, married forever to the blackness of infinite space in the massive window alongside.

The television screens had been a last minute addition by Wallace Rushford-Sale. It had occurred to him that if he was going to be drifting through the void for all eternity, while still with the somewhat restricted power of sight, it would be a shame to be entirely cut off from what was happening back with the good old human race, cunts though they generally were. As such he had demanded the installation of a widescreen television, tuned permanently to CNN, so that he could keep tabs on the progress, or inevitable decline, of civilization. "Keep tabs on" is the wrong expression obviously, but nonetheless he wanted to be able to see all the major events; when the one-hundredth President of the United States was sworn into office, that man's smiling face of false promise would parade in front of his eyes as though solely for the benefit of Wallace Rushford-Sale, isolated in oblivion, and none of his old classmates or work colleagues would be able to lay claim to similar.

There had been a couple of days of critical indecision, when Wallace Rushford-Sale had questioned himself on whether or not to opt instead for a DVD player showing repeats of his favourite sitcom; ultimately though he decided to be virtuous and stick with the news coverage. He had also considered whether or not it would be a sensible precaution to take some erotic distraction with him on his journey, to help fill the emptier stretches of time, and to compensate for the lack of female contact, a more intense version of a similar void he had already experienced back on Earth; hence the addition of the second television screen, aka the Grumbletron9000. Wallace Rushford-Sale had stipulated that this additional request be made after his death, or deactivation as the crew referred to it, so as to avoid any potential embarrassment on his part. This, it might be argued, was the one factor of the arrangement that Wallace Rushford-Sale did think through in advance.

There was no power devoted to steering or propelling the capsule forward; the pod was launched into space attached to a shuttle already heading out on another arguably more important mission, and once pointing in vaguely the right direction (by Wallace Rushford-Sale's

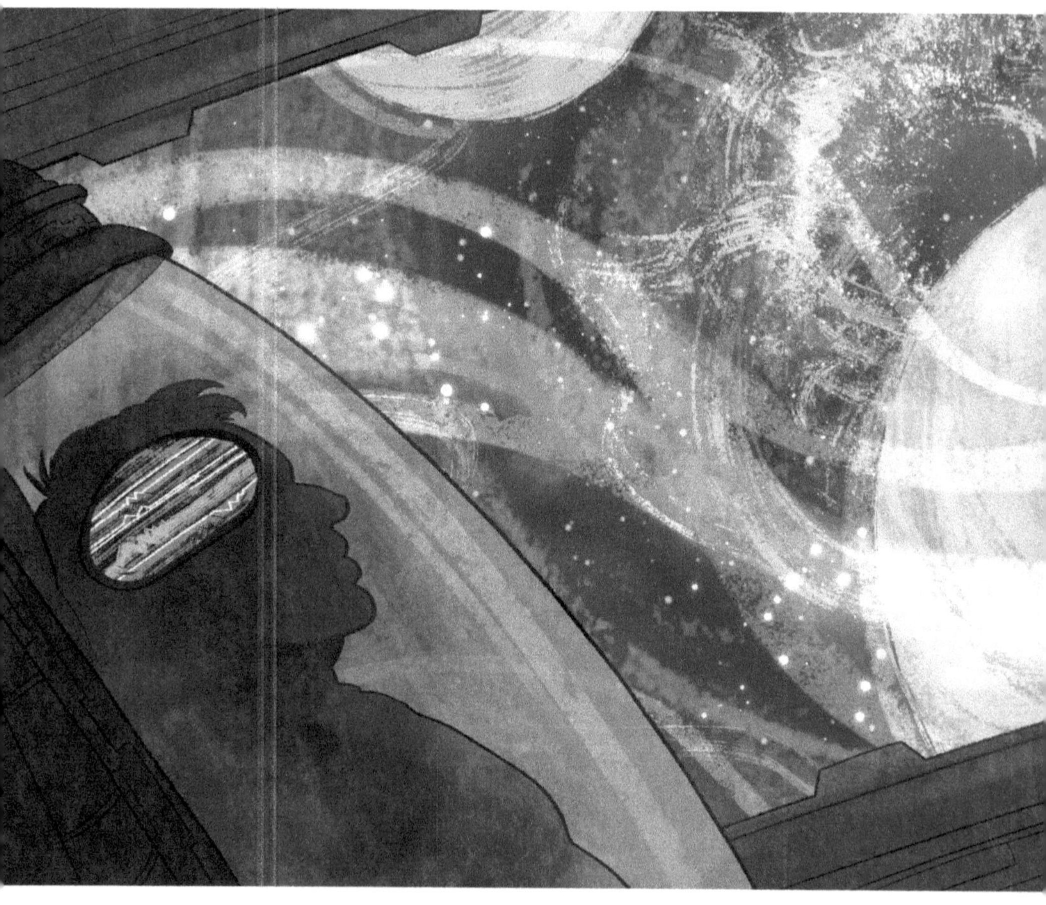

instructions, anywhere so long as away from the Sun), the pod was detached and left to drift whichever way it pleased. The installation of some sort of intercom had been raised, considered, and promptly dismissed by Wallace Rushford-Sale, on the grounds that he would be unable to communicate with anybody, or to hear anyone trying to contact him. Subsequently all power in the capsule was directed into the two television screens, as well as the handful of LED lights on the console deemed absolutely necessary by the maintenance team.

In order to conserve this power for as long as possible, Wallace Rushford-Sale had requested some sort of mechanism to turn on the news channel for one hour every ten years; this, he figured, would give him a regular update on events without missing too much of any great long-term significance. Concerning the Grumbletron9000, Wallace Rushford-Sale had demanded somewhat less frugally, and again posthumously, that the video be switched on for ten minutes every twenty-four hours. Had he made this order while still cerebral, the crew would probably have tried to talk him out of this, underlining the pointlessness of playing dirty videos for a man with no sex drive, or desire for anything whatsoever; but this would have been too awkward a conversation for Wallace Rushford-Sale to navigate without major incident.

Of the total time spent in actually thinking about this project in any depth, Wallace Rushford-Sale had probably invested most of his thought into the naming of the ship, and after much humming and indecision, he had eventually decided on the Cro-Magnon XIX. He had initially aimed for something more traditional of naming spacecrafts, perusing countless books on Greek mythology for inspiration, but the name Cro-Magnon had stuck with him, from something he had seen in a magazine somewhere, and consulting the definition in the dictionary, he found it suitably fitting to his purpose, not to mention its grand and intimidating sound; the affixed XIX had no significance, and was only chosen for aesthetic purposes. Unfortunately for Wallace Rushford-Sale, he had given the designated name to the crew only moments before his shutdown, and the man responsible for painting the name on the side of the craft clearly had no knowledge of prehistoric civilizations. Subsequently, as Wallace Rushford-Sale's inanimate body was borne through the glass doors to the ship, the words "Crow Magnum Xix" shone down darkly on his immobile eyes; clearly Roman numerals had not been part of the crew member's school curriculum either, as the XIX had clearly been painted as letters. Had Wallace Rushford-Sale's brother Francis survived the car crash in 2009, and still been alive to witness the loading of his brother beneath this magnificent typo, he might have said something to his wife (who at this point had still been alive, but for her own reasons was not present for the occasion) about it sounding like the fraternity house of a particularly poor university, or something similarly disparaging. Fortunately though, Francis Rushford-Sale was dead, as for all intents and purposes, was his brother Wallace.

It is impossible for us to speculate, of course, but it is probably safe to say that the power in the capsule did not last quite as long as Wallace Rushford-Sale might have hoped. Having caught the second of his ten-yearly episodes of mankind's current events, CNN promptly changed their programming to a different channel setting, resulting in three ensuing hours of blue glaze over the next thirty years before the electricity in the pod ran out. The Grumbletron9000 could possibly be blamed for the rapid consumption of power, of course; but had it not been for CNN's relocation to another station, Wallace Rushford-Sale would still have been able to see incoming forty-eighth President Aaron James Killpatrick place his hand on the Washington Bible, before the picture puffed out for good.

So had passed the best part of a century in near total darkness, with an occasional float of colour through the window, and the initial white and blue flares from the TV screens. There were endless stars outside, of course, as well as a farewell tidal wave of purple and green as he left the galaxy. Wallace Rushford-Sale had wondered aloud, prior to his departure, whether it would be possible for the pod to rotate on an axis, thus enabling him to see as much and miss as little as possible during his flight. The crew had replied that they couldn't see how this might be achieved, without completely redesigning the craft and investing a lot more time, money and power into it, said power being by necessity diverted away from the all-important television screens. As it turned out though, the pod seemed to spin quite well of its own accord. There may have been a couple of times when something might have passed behind the windowless side of the pod, where Wallace Rushford-Sale was forever secured, but he would not have known this, or been able to experience any regret if he had. Everything was just colour: black, white, yellow, blue, plus some other hues that people back on Earth would not be familiar with.

At this particular point a long white shape hovers into the window frame, and a large glass bubble holding two pink faces enters the blank vision of Wallace Rushford-Sale. How clearly these appear in his eyes is uncertain; it had not occurred to Wallace Rushford-Sale to include some sort of equipment to periodically rinse his eyes, in lieu of the ability to blink, nor did he know whether this would even be required. He figured there would be very little dust in a vacuum-sealed ship, and even fewer flies and such, so he had decided in the end to leave it. Were anyone looking into his eyes though, such as the two pink faces outside are now trying to do, they might notice a sort of crystalline look about them, not unlike quartz; whether this was a film of something on his eyes, the result of years of unfocussed staring, or simply the lack of a human mind, no-one would be able to say.

Even with liquid clear vision though, Wallace Rushford-Sale would still be unable to read the expression on these two faces, let alone read the words Perseus 7 painted on the white. He is completely oblivious to the hello entering his chamber, can you hear us in there. For all these two blobs may talk about themselves, or where they had come from, their home lives and families, they remain nothing more than specks on an unrecorded timeline. The only thing that Wallace Rushford-Sale registers from this meeting is that first monochrome shift from one to the other, followed by the sudden return of black as the white moves away.

Of course, all of this is just speculation on our part. No one can say for certain what Wallace Rushford-Sale now feels or doesn't feel; although the maintenance crew, were they still alive today, would be of the firm opinion that he is not feeling anything. If he is still alive and even remotely cognizant, Wallace Rushford-Sale may have seen things that you and I can't even begin to imagine; if he is really, in the scientific and ultimate sense of the word, dead, he will probably know whether or not there is an afterlife. Wallace Rushford-Sale may have sailed to the end of the universe by now, or even beyond; he may have been sucked into orbit and spent countless decades circling the same dead lump of ashen rock.

Wherever he turns now, and whatever his circumstances, Wallace Rushford-Sale obviously did not think this through properly. He thought about it, obviously, but he didn't really think; he certainly isn't thinking now, or so we might think. He didn't even think to install a self-destruct mechanism. Not that he would be able to use it if he had.

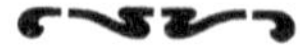

New Year's Eve: 65,000,000 B.C.

Mike Algera

Long ago there was this monster who roamed the earth. He was a listless giant with physical deformities. He came from nowhere, and had no home to go to. He was alone. He was constantly searching. Even though he had no home, no loved ones, no purpose, he wandered aimlessly.

One day, he was sitting on a rock with his head in his hands. He stared out into the distant trees and mountains. The breeze was calm and the sun warmed his skin, but it brought him no comfort. It was near this same rock he met a dinosaur. The dinosaur happened to be stomping along, when he spotted the rock and the monster slouching atop of it out of the corner of his eye.

He knelt down close to the monster till his massive eye was level to the monster's monstrous face and asked: "Hey monster…where do you come from, and why do you look so glum?"

The monster heaved a tremendous sigh.

"As far back as I can remember," he said. "I've lived as long as the earth. I don't know where I came from, but I was made by a scientist."

"What's a scientist? And why did he make you?"

"I don't know. All I know is that he made me, with the help of lightning. And I'm glum because like the earth, I don't sleep. My body can't find rest, no matter the time of day I can't find sleep. Not even at night."

The longer the dinosaur listened to the monster's troubles the more he sympathized.

"I can relate," said the dinosaur. "All I can say is someone made me too. And for whatever purpose I can't say. All I know is that I'm always hungry and therefore, always awake. Everywhere I go, I eat things. Living things mind you, like other dinosaurs and people."

"Everywhere I go, I always end up being scary. At night, whenever I approach a pack of sleeping beasts, upon my coming they stir from slumber, turn to panic and flee."

"Yeah, I end up being scary too! It makes me so mad! This is probably

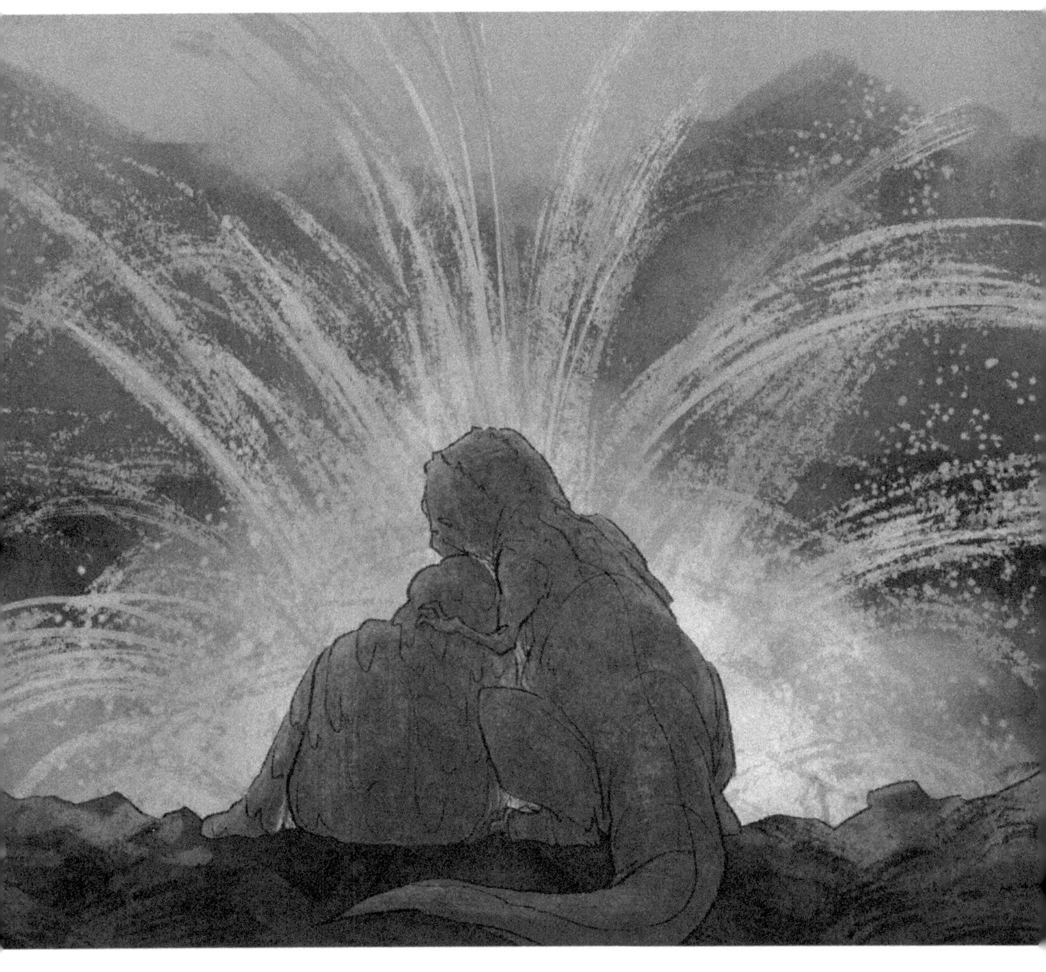

why I eat."

It was after this statement the monster perked up. The two fell silent for a long while. They had so much in common, it didn't matter how much time had passed, so long as they remained in each other's company.

Suddenly, the monster was struck with a thought. He asked the dinosaur if he was still hungry.

"Nope," the dinosaur replied. "I've lost my appetite."

"You mean you don't wish to eat me?"

"Eat you? Why would I do that?"

Then it dawned on the dinosaur that something unearthly had happened.

"I've lost my appetite!"

"Then if talking to me," said the monster, "resulted in you losing your appetite, perhaps if you talk to me some more, maybe I'll fall asleep."

It took some time for the monster's plan to sink into the dinosaur's brain, but the longer the monster explained, demonstrated, and re-explained his plan, the less famished the dinosaur became. When at long last the dinosaur understood, he asked what they should talk about.

"Let's talk about each other. After all, it was this same subject that helped you lose your appetite…so, why change the subject?"

"Yeah, I liked talking about each other. Let's talk some more on that subject!"

After much excitement, the two continued their conversation. They talked and talked about each other with great interest. The dinosaur remained less famished; however, sleep didn't come to the monster.

"This isn't working," cried the monster. "Let's change the subject."

"To what?"

"Anything…"

The subject of the conversation changed. Some time later it was changed again. Still, sleep didn't come to the monster.

"This isn't working! I don't understand why I'm still awake. You lost your appetite, why can't I gain sleep?"

"Maybe we could talk about things on earth that are always asleep?"

The dinosaur's suggestion puzzled the monster.

"Could there be anything on earth that's always asleep?"

They both pondered this quandary. The dinosaur scratched his head with his tail and shrugged, "The volcano is pretty much always asleep. It's hardly ever awake."

"Where is the volcano?"

"Oh, it's over there. See?"

The dinosaur's tail pointed to the distant horizon where the mountains sloped beyond the valley. As it turned out, the volcano was opposite where the mountains resided.

"Well, if I'm to get sleep and you're to stay less famished, we must go visit the volcano."

"Great! Climb up my back, and we'll go together!"

Delighted, the monster climbed up the dinosaur's back and the two companions started their journey towards the volcano. Along the way the trees timbered; living things, dinosaurs, people and the like scattered and fled, not daring to interfere with the two companions' quest. Day and night they tarried, their prattle and pursuit of the volcano tireless.

On December 31, 65,000,000 B.C., they reached their destination. They stood on the lip of the volcano and peered down its cavernous mouth.

The dinosaur asked, "What now?"

"I don't know. Maybe, you should ask it to wake up."

"What do I say?"

"Say, 'volcano wake up!'"

The dinosaur did as he was bid. Nothing happened.

The monster then suggested, "Say, 'volcano, are you awake?'"

The dinosaur nodded and asked the volcano if it was awake, and waited. There was no reply.

"What now?"

"I'll say, 'volcano wake up,' and you say, 'volcano, are you awake?'"

The two companions agreed: one urged the volcano to awaken, the other persisted in asking if it was awake. This went on for some time until one suggested they switch commands. The latter went on till nightfall and at that moment a terrific lightning storm rippled through the sky.

Observing this terrific sight, the monster concluded: "The lightning! Perhaps *It* shall stir the volcano."

A bolt of lightning flashed across the seething sky; its brilliant streak of light like the naked limb of a white oak tree, tumbled down and smacked the lip of the volcano, which cracked and crumbled into a sore. The volcano swallowed fragments of itself and in so doing, its gaping pit gurgled to life. The monster and the dinosaur were blinded by a red glow and a belch of heat.

"It's so hot…I can barely open my eyes!"

"Me too," the monster chimed in.

The heat was too much for the monster, and his body gave out from fatigue.

"Hey, you look tired!" said the dinosaur. "You look like you're about to fall asleep."

"Yeah…" the monster tried to stifle a yawn. "I think I could lie down, right here…right now."

"Me too…"

The two companions retired on the volcano's lip, the dinosaur lay on his side while the monster lay down to sleep, his feet dangling above the volcano's mouth.

"Goodnight," said the monster.

"Goodnight," said the dinosaur.

Then they both talked till the dinosaur became enveloped by a blanket of magma. The night was warm and still. Sleep at long last came to the monster.

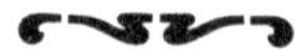

Killed By Shadows

Charlotte Unsworth

discovered the cure by accident; Ben insisted I go to the park with them, said it wasn't good for me to stay in the house. I finally gave in; maybe he was getting suspicious I wasn't going out and, after all, if I went I could keep Simon away from anyone who looked sick, or tainted. I didn't know why I hadn't thought of it before! He needed me to go. We hadn't been out in so long. It was Saturday afternoon and people were out, walking dogs, playing ball, feeding ducks. For a while it seemed everything was normal, and nobody was worried. It was a glorious clear day and nobody seemed to have the dark shadow clinging to them. Ben pulled half a loaf of bread from his rucksack. "Knew you just needed to get out of the house." And I was smiling, properly smiling, and I started to feel as though I could put the shadowy sickness in my head alongside measles, whooping cough, TB. Real, dangerous, but so remote I needn't worry. Too far away to be any real danger.

Then, as Simon was leaning out as far as he could to throw bread for the ducks, I saw it just a few feet away. He came from nowhere. While I had been congratulating myself and letting my guard down, he had come up to the muddy riverbank with his own bag of breadcrumbs and a darkening shroud surrounding him. He too leaned as far as he could but didn't have a watching father to hold him back. He tipped forward, him and his shadow. Ben grabbed Simon back and leapt in after the boy. I clung to our son while his father swam the child back to the shore. The boy wasn't breathing. I wanted to call out—don't touch him, stay away, don't risk infection, but Simon was clinging to me and it happened so fast. As Ben leaned over, giving mouth to mouth and pounding his chest, I saw nothing but the boy. The shadow was gone.

The boy was fine. He came back to life spluttering and coughing as an ambulance screamed up to us. Ben was congratulated and thanked. We went home, looked after our son with a little more tenderness. I'm sure Ben was thinking about what could have been if he hadn't leapt in, or hadn't had hold of Simon's coat. I was thinking about the shadow and how it disappeared when the boy was in danger. Could that be the key to getting them to leave? I missed being able to just walk out of the door without worrying. It was everything I hadn't wanted when I became pregnant, to be cut off from the world like this, but once he was here I was responsible for him, and I had to keep him safe inside.

I dwelt on it for days, thinking about how to make sure that someone else knew how to save these children rather than condemn them to the half-life I saw all around me. I was sure by then they were being attacked; I wrote to everyone I could think of, sitting at the kitchen table while Ben was at work, and felt for the first time since Simon was born that I was useful in some way other than simply being his mother. Ben didn't believe me. Even though we hadn't spoken about it since before I went to Isobel's, I still caught him watching me as if he didn't trust me. I had to be very careful. I told him I was still going to the baby groups, still meeting Isobel, still trying to be as normal as possible. In the letters, I was as matter of fact as I could be; if I appeared hysterical or overwrought they'd never do anything but throw them away as the ramblings of a scared mother.

There was no response at all.

When I sat, later, in the hospital watching the children it should have been hard not to feel angry about being ignored while I had vital information. But they watched me take medication to dull those feelings. Even with Ben I didn't know what to say. The emotion was just gone, wrapped in cotton wool so thick I couldn't get to it anymore. I know he made an effort to talk to me, but he struggled to forget. He doesn't understand. I was so afraid when I finally saw the mist starting to grow around Simon. He was in the garden and I thought it was a smear on the window or a cloud overhead but when I went to the door, I knew. All my protection and he still got infected as if it was some childish rebellion to prove I couldn't look after him. Ben insisted on putting him to bed, not ruining their routine time together. He said it was nothing. He said Simon barely felt warm and I shouldn't panic so much, with that clipped tone that sometimes creeps in. The next morning Simon seemed perfectly happy, but I could see the cloud growing around him. Ben couldn't see it, couldn't even feel a temperature. At least I had had time to think, to plan what I needed to do. I thought I had planned it so carefully.

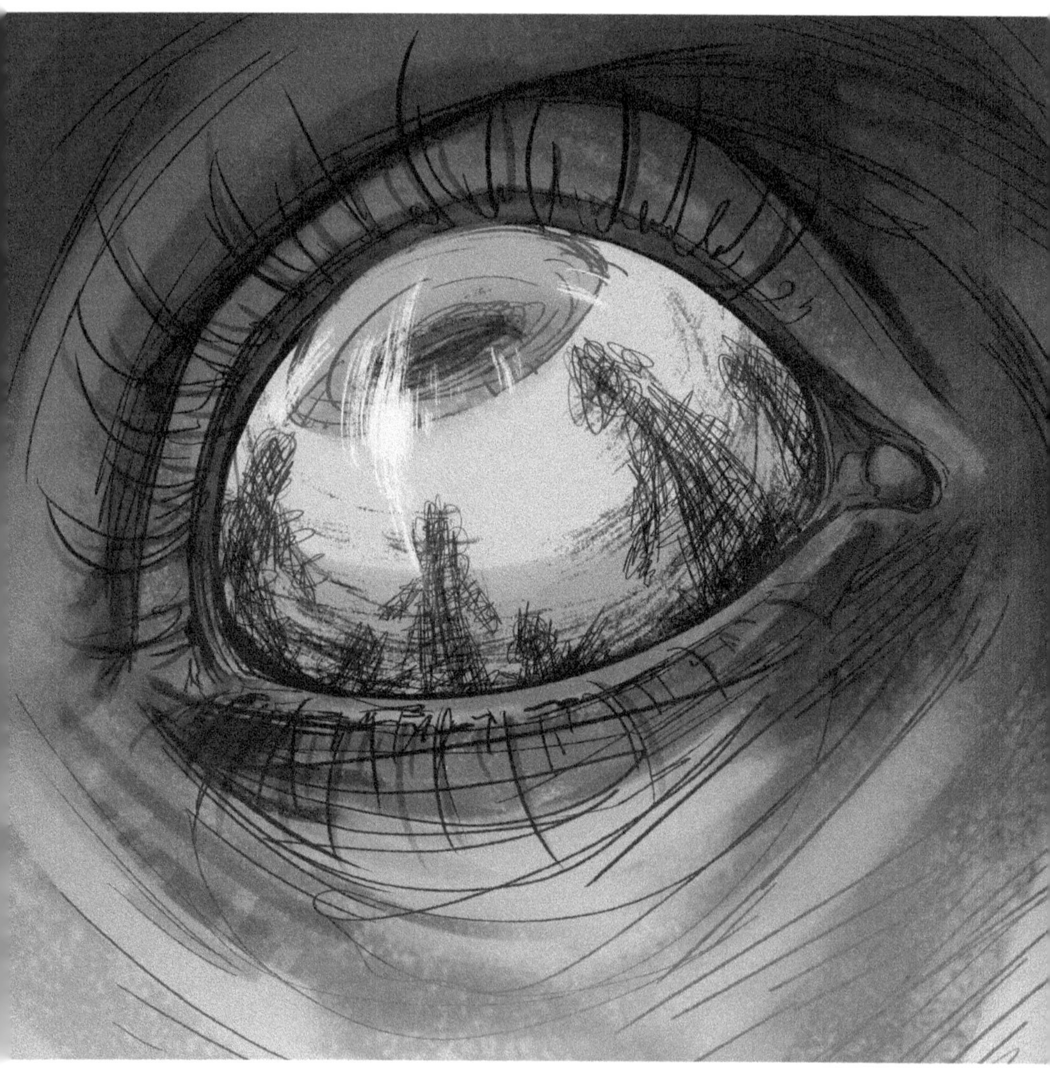

When I was in the hospital I longed to go home, missing my own patch of grass and my own living room, my things around me. I knew what they wanted—answer their questions, take their pills, forget the shadows. I couldn't see them anymore. It should have been easier, meaning they were really gone and the end of the sickness was near. When the shadows faded it should have been because the children were winning the fight against their infection. But they didn't disappear completely, not at first. So when they did, I knew I was being blinded, their drugs stopping me from seeing what was there. I tried to accept they were gone and be relieved, like they wanted. I followed their schedule—walked, read, sat outside—and expected any minute someone would call me a liar. More often the book lay open, unread on the arm of the sofa. I turned a page every so often so anyone watching would think I was reading, but I watched the children.

They were sick.

Even though I couldn't see it I could see in the way they sat, glazed and silent, but I couldn't see the shadows around them. If even I couldn't see them anymore, how could anyone help them? I knew what would. The boy in the park proved it to me. I had tried to cure Simon, and so nearly succeeded. I knew how to cure them.

Over and over I was told to think logically. Doctors, counsellors, Ben. They all said the same thing. Think logically. And, logically, before I tried, I needed to be sure that they had the shadow sickness, not something else. I stopped taking the pills. It took some doing, hiding them under my tongue. When the sugar coating dissolved, bitterness crumpled my face and my throat tensed to avoid retching. But I needed to be able to see them. I halved the dose and soon felt like myself, alert and normal.

I was careful; too much of a change and the doctors would become suspicious. So when Ben visited, I kept my face slack. I nodded and smiled just enough, and listened to his talk. We never talked about Simon, and I was glad Ben didn't bring him up; I couldn't have kept my composure if we did. The downside of feeling everything was that I felt his absence almost more than when I first arrived. Once when Ben left I couldn't help myself, clinging to him. He stared at me. Was it my sudden emotion or my touch that made him jump? I hugged him instead, trying to turn the loss of control into something planned, expected. Normal.

I stopped taking the drugs and my vision started to slowly return. I wished it hadn't. There were more shadows than I ever thought possible, they had grown, become multitudes and I started to doubt whether I could make any difference. I saw so few children from my window vantage-point and yet they were almost blackened in shadow. I knew then what I was up against. They couldn't wait for me any longer.

I found where they were thickest. The nurses said the desire to do something was a good sign and encouraged me to walk in the garden outside the double doors at the top of the grass, where I could watch the patients and visitors, where they came from and where they went. I had to wait, until they were giving out afternoon medication and I held mine in my mouth, before I could slip away. It took just a few minutes to follow them up the ramp, down the hall, across the glass-windowed corridor, and then back. I waited for the sword to fall but nobody had noticed. The children's ward had been closer than I thought. All afternoon, I waited for someone to ask what I had been doing, for the doctors to come for me. Nobody said anything, nobody tried to stop me. They must have seen me. Busy as they were, the nurses must have noticed what I was doing. That they hadn't said anything, they let me go, told me that finally someone believed me. They were trying to help.

Once I had the silent approval of the nurses I knew I could focus. No matter what I did, in my head I could see what would happen. While I thought and prepared I gathered materials. Even with the nurses' agreement I couldn't ask them; I knew ours had to be a silent compact but it became easier to collect what I needed and I was grateful to them for helping in what small ways they could. I collected it all in a duffle bag under my bed as carefully as I had packed away the photo album Ben brought and the first stuffed toy Simon was bought. It grew, and I practiced in my head, over and over, seeing everything that could go wrong until I got it right every time. I was ready.

Nighttime routines in hospitals are never-changing. I lay in bed fully dressed and hidden by the sheets, like a teenager waiting for a forbidden party. I waited with my eyes shut, visualizing success. When the nurse walked in, she didn't come across to me, just left the door slightly open; even though she couldn't speak to encourage me, I knew what she was telling me: it was time to go. She returned to her office as usual, giving me time enough to do what was necessary. I lifted my duffle bag. The hallway was bright after the darkness of my room, but I kept going, following the bright lines on the floor to show visitors the way.

Securing the doors was louder than I hoped, damaging the magnetic catch that unlocked them and blocking the entrance as best I could. I dragged around furniture, thankful it had wheels, but some squeaked so loudly I had to abandon them for fear the children would wake and, with them, the shadows. I had imagined that happening so many times but never been able to envisage what they would do. Sometimes I thought they would withdraw, admiring my courage in saving their victims. Other times, I had nightmares of being swallowed whole by the viscous blackness.

The fires were unexpectedly easy to start. I had thought they would be difficult but it is surprising how much flammable liquid there is in a hospital, especially when nurses leave their keys unattended for five minutes to allow you into the cleaning cupboard. There is only so much you can take from the trolley when it stops outside the door, but the cupboard held huge bottles and so many of them that I could easily take one or two without them being missed. Hand sanitizer burns with a lovely blue flame. Although my trembling made it difficult to light the matches, the sheets covered in it lit so quickly I had to hurry to pile on more fabric to keep the flames burning. Any moment the shadows would realize they were being threatened and that they couldn't win; by the time security broke in and doused the flames the shadows would have fled and the children would be safe.

The mixture of bleach and ammonia I poured around the room started to have its noxious effect, mixing with the black fog that was starting to fill the room. The smell and smoke made me retch; I stumbled and fell onto one of the beds, grabbing at the rail. The girl in it was stirring already, roused by the heat in the room, and my movement was the last needle to draw her out of sleep and into the nightmare around her. I could see her starting to panic, her hair matted with sleep and her face quickly losing all signs of the drowsiness with which she first looked at me. She opened her mouth, to scream or shout for help or ask me what I was doing there, but instead smoke gushed into her lungs and she choked, rough coughing that tore at her throat. Her gasps only made it worse as with every attempt to breathe she drew in more of the fumes. She reached out for me. The shadow around her grew weaker and I seized my opportunity. I took one of her hands in mine and, with the other, held closed her mouth and nose. It took only a few minutes; the shadows disappeared and she slipped back into sleep, falling onto the pillow again. She would wake when security guards crashed into the room and then, she would be safe.

One by one the shadows were losing, fading into the smoke that filled the room. They would be here any minute, leaving us just long enough to let the shadows be destroyed and then they would come through the door and put the fire out. I could hear them banging on the door, shouting to be let in—but I knew they had to wait just a few minutes more. Just a few, and then we would be safe. The metal rail on the side of the bed was getting hot. I held her hand, and thought about how Simon's tiny hands had reached for mine. Then I had been so angry—he couldn't understand. He was too young to know I was trying to help him. All he could feel were my hands. I think he knew I was doing the best I could for him as I pressed down, as I had for her. The shadows fought me. They faded but I was slipping too, choked with smoke. The banging on the door got louder, a fire alarm cried through the corridors, and the flames roared, but my vision went black before the firefighters came in.

Ben told me, later, that they found me slumped across the girl as if I was protecting her. He thought that, like with Simon, it was my fault and wanted to tell himself that I had changed my mind at the last minute. He never understood but I couldn't have let those things take him without trying to protect him. He told me that the children were safe now. He means from me. The shadows might have gone from those children—I will never know—but they know that I know about them. I can't see them. The medicine runs directly into tubes in my body that I can't control. Everything is closing in, shutting me down and wrapping me in unfeeling so that I feel nothing, but I can feel myself slipping into it and I cling to care. But I can't see them. I lie in my new bed, in the new hospital I have been moved to, and try to hear them. At night is when I think I can almost hear them whisper and creak outside the door like the wind in trees or the crackle of smoke. I am sure they are there, still, but nobody will ever again let me try to save us from them.

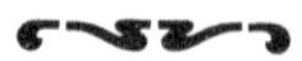

The Japanese Rice Cooker

Jhon Sanchez

For Yuknow

From: Richard Cook richcook2000@gmail.com
To: Nagano Kurimoto Appliances, Inc.
customerservice@naganokurimoto.com

Dear Sir or Madam:

Last December 1st, I got a Century GenRice Cooker because my wife asked for a divorce. I bought my own appliances and moved out of my home to an apartment nearby. This rice cooker is a dream. I have never had a bad batch of rice in all the different types I made: long-grain brown, medium-grain brown, white Basmati, brown Basmati or Jasmine. I set the timer in the morning, so the rice cooks while I am at work. One day, when I got to the apartment, my wife was waiting for me in front of the door with the divorce papers. Inside, my place smelled of cooked rice, which my wife found surprisingly pleasant. Right then, she too fell in love with this rice cooker and began to come by to eat rice with me every night. The pot makes a cute little ring when the cooking cycle starts and ends, which almost always makes her smile. Since five days ago, I moved back home and we are not planning to divorce anymore. Simply put, since we got this rice cooker, we have more time for us, we are saving money and even eating more nutritiously. We have only one question. After the rice cooks, I find faces. The rice forms faces: two holes for the eyes, two holes for the nostrils, and a smile. I have seen other happy faces in the remains of my black coffee, but I have never seen it in a rice pot until I bought this cooker. I was wondering if this is normal?

Thanks for your consideration in this matter,
Richard Cook
126 S. Meridian Street, Apt. 11 B
Indianapolis, Indiana 46203

PS: Yesterday, my wife said that she loves me more than ever and she would never divorce me, but God knows. If she ever leaves me, she can keep the house, the car, the retirement fund but not my rice cooker.

Quick Question ☺
Wed, Dec 20, 2013 at 5:39 PM

```
From: Katherine Wells Katwells@aol.com
To: Nagano Kurimoto Appliances
customerservice@naganokurimoto.com
```

Dear Sir or Madam:

I grew tired of cooking rice and having the burned crust at the bottom of the pan, so I splurged on this rice cooker. This machine rocks! My rice is always fluffy, tender and never mushy. From now on, I won't even try the rice that comes with the orders from Chinese restaurants. It is SUPER easy to use and clean. (I don't need a sponge.) But, I think I may have to play with the rice-to-water ratio to find the perfect texture for brown rice, and to avoid the strange images in the cooked rice. I probably should have gotten the next biggest size, so I could have leftovers (Duh, how can I make fried rice if I don't have leftovers?). I think I overfill it. Maybe this is the reason I see the sailboat-like image on the top of the rice. My husband, who is an engineer, says that this image is only a feature. He says that it is a kind of logo that your company has designed to form in the cooked rice. I have to admit, it is quite beautiful—a white rice boat with a headsail, a mainsail and a mast. My husband says that it resembles a sloop, but I wouldn't know about that. I think it is only a coincidence of putting too much water and/or rice. Could you clarify this for me? I am sorry to bother you. Maybe it is just a stupid question. I don't want you to feel that I am dissatisfied; on the contrary, I just love this kitchen gadget. The jasmine rice is so good that I can't stop eating it.

We are moving to the Netherlands next month (My husband got a scholarship to study at Maastricht University). Our new address will be:
Katherine Wells
Leidenlaan 18-20
6229 EZ Maastricht, Netherlands

I still don't know if I will have the same e-mail address, so just in case, I will write to you again. I hope I'm not bothering you.
Thanks,
Katherine Wells
219 Union Street, Apt. 3A
Brooklyn, NY 11225

PS: I already packed our rice cooker!

Technical Support Requested/ 6th E-MAIL!
Wed, Dec 20, 2013 at 7:14 PM

From: Joe Zambrano JoeZamba@yahoo.com
To: Nagano Kurimoto Appliances
customerservice@naganokurimoto.com

This is the sixth e-mail I have written regarding this issue. I don't think this item is a disappointment; I think the only con is the bad translation from Japanese into English. The first time I used this rice cooker was Halloween, and I saw that the rice, after cooking, took the shape of a skull with two bones at the bottom. My sister, Miranda, and I had organized a Halloween party, and the rice cooker became a sensation. After that, the rice always took the same shape. Some of my friends even became scared (Funny!). I have looked at the instruction manual as to how to change the settings. Christmas is coming up, and

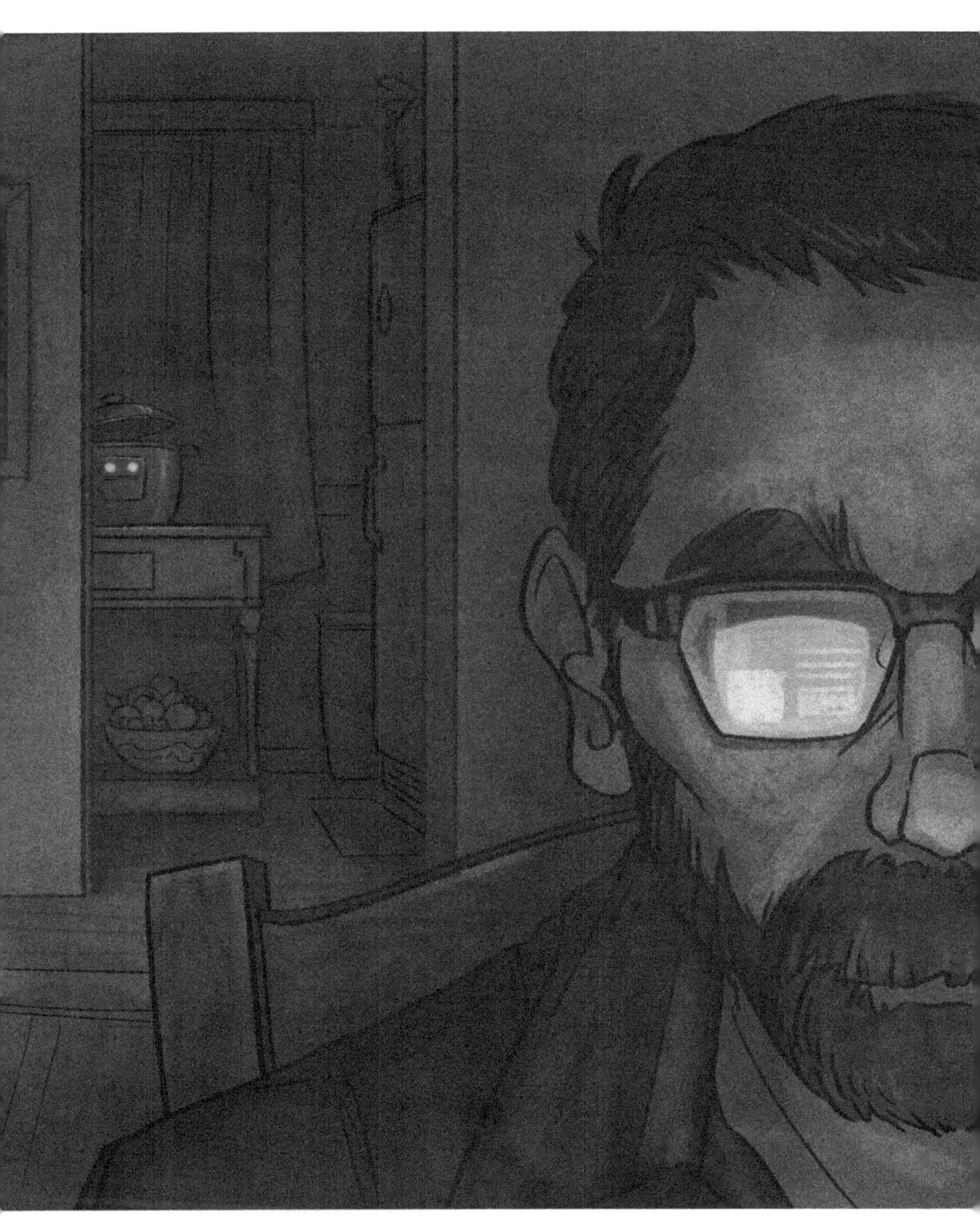

I want to have the image of white pine trees in my rice. I already called technical support just before Thanksgiving, but to no avail. I have played with all the buttons, and I even cut the water by 25 percent, but I always get the same skull. The cooker plays a happy tune when the rice is done, but I would rather have music that is appropriate to the occasion. I want to have a pine tree or Santa Claus along with a Christmas carol. Today is already December 20th, and I want to surprise my friends with the rice image. Why is this so complicated for you? What kind of customer service is this?

Joe Zambrano
46-17 47th Street
Sunnyside, NY 11101

Claim # 334655 / RE: Miranda Zambrano
Fri, January 14, 2014 at 1:04 PM

```
From: Nagano Kurimoto Appliances
customerservice@naganokurimoto.com
To: Miranda Zambrano Miramirazam@hotmail.com
```

Dear Mrs. Zambrano,

Thank you for sharing your concerns regarding the death of Mr. Zambrano. On behalf of Nagano Kurimoto Appliances, Inc., I want to express my sincere condolences for the loss of your brother. I certainly understand your feelings, as described during your phone calls to our customer service representative line. We are privileged to provide the best quality appliances in the world to our distinctive customers. Our products pass the highest tests of safety to meet the needs of a diverse customer base. So, your comments were taken very seriously and their insinuation, very disheartening.

I understand that you feel that Mr. Zambrano's death was caused by some kind of malfunction of our Century GenRice Cooker. I certainly would like to thank you for sending Mr. Zambrano's rice cooker to

Japan. A special group of engineers inspected the rice cooker, and found no malfunction whatsoever in the appliance. Our team provided a detailed report, which is available to you and to your attorneys upon request. In our Yamamoto and Nakagawa laboratories, we performed tests of iron concentration, polymer solidification, and electrical shock, among others. In all these tests, Mr. Zambrano's rice cooker worked perfectly.

I requested that a statement be forwarded to the customer service agents, through their immediate manager, who failed to respond to Mr. Zambrano's communications. Mr. Zambrano wrote six e-mails dated: November 5th, November 12th, November 23rd, December 4th, December 18th, and December 20th. Mr. Zambrano also called technical support on more than one occasion, requesting instructions on setting his rice cooker to make a different image than that of a skull. Unfortunately, our customer service agents did not understand the nature of his request. The Century GenRice cooker is a kitchen device that enables its users to taste the best rice in the world. We do not understand how our rice cooker could produce an image in the shape of a skull. The customer service agent should have replied as such or tried to uncover the true nature of Mr. Zambrano's requests.

We are truly sorry that you found your brother dead, close to the rice cooker, with warm rice in his mouth; this does not, however, mean to imply that the appliance has a malfunction.

That being said, I am very sorry for not answering Mr. Zambrano's letters on time, but know that we were in the process of answering them. I understand you are requesting compensation for your brother's death. However, his death was not caused by the use, or a malfunction of, our Century GenRice Cooker. I am sorry to disappoint you, as I understand that this is not the answer you were expecting.

Again, I hope you will accept my sincere regrets for your loss and my assurance that this incident has been addressed thoroughly.

I hope this information is helpful. Your satisfaction is our business, and Nagano Kurimoto Appliances, Inc. always attempts to not only

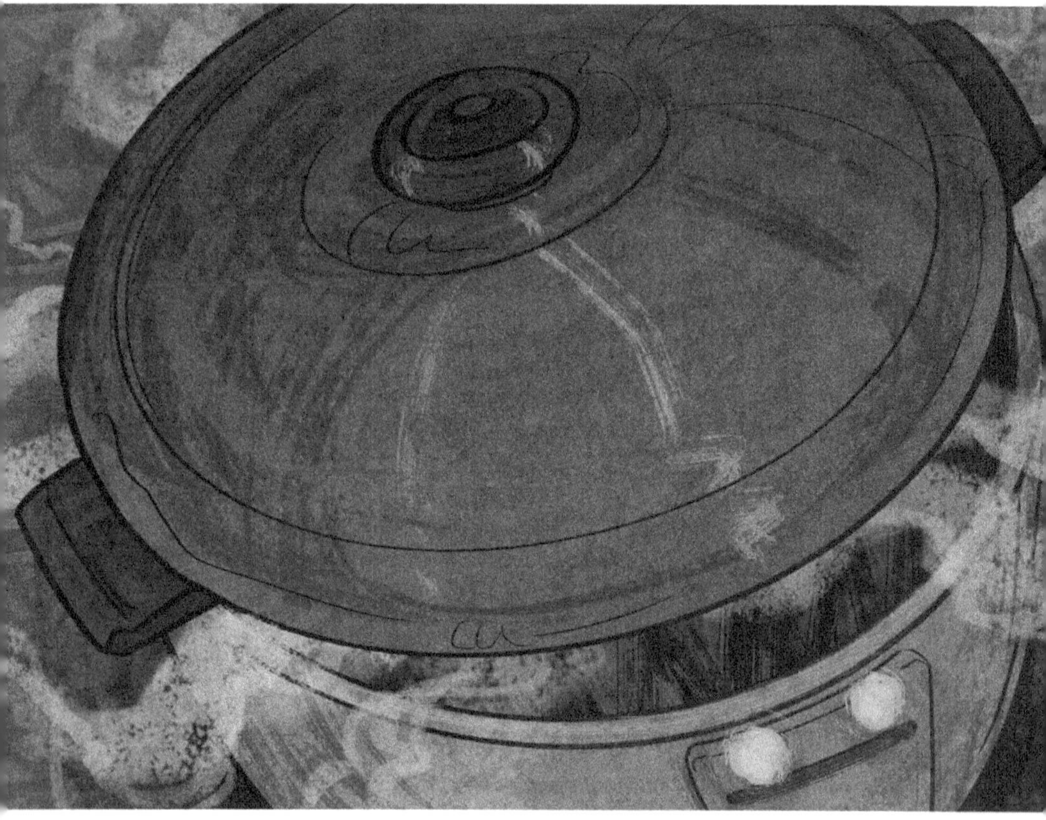

meet, but exceed, our customers' expectations.

Sincerely,
Yakiko Murota
Coordinator Customer Care
2 - 8 - 1 2 Minami-Azabu,
Minato, Tokyo 106-0047, Japan
Phone: +81 3-5447-7800
Fax: +81 3-5447-9988

IRREGULARITIES
March 19, 2014 at 2:01 PM

From: Yakiko Murota, Coordinator Customer Care
Ymurota@naganokurimoto.com
To: Suto Nagano, Vice-president Commercial
Relations Snagano@naganokurimoto.com

Mr. Nagano,

Even though I have only held this position for six months, I am deeply concerned about the future of your family's company, now a global corporation. In these short months, I have received multiple messages and letters from all over world, mostly praising the quality of our appliances. There are, however, some messages coming out from America particularly different from any others. You have been made aware of the case of Joe Zambrano, whose sister made a claim for his death. Other e-mails consistently described a variety of images appearing in the rice after it is cooked, as reported by Mr. Zambrano, Richard Cook and Katherine Wells, to name a few. Their correspondence has been attached.

On a more recent situation, Shake the Shake, a neighborhood juice store in Brooklyn, New York, sued another vendor, The Alternative Juice Jews, in the Second Circuit of New York. The complaint states that The Alternative Juice Jews used our exclusive Super Bionic

Blender to drive Shake the Shake to bankruptcy. Alternative had started to light a candle on the lid of their blenders that, according to Shake, caused sour flavoring to develop in their juices at their location across the street. Shake stores hired an expert, a kind of witch who is willing to testify that our blender can transmit voodoo energy causing the clientele of competitors to run away.

Coincidentally, yesterday, I got a letter from a woman in El Paso, Texas, Mrs. Maruja Martínez, who described herself as a medium. She wants to obtain the exclusive license to our Coffee Machine Great Brew Beans because its particular noise during the percolation process is in reality "a language from another world." She claims that she can interpret the language and people have already started to come for sessions to hear our coffee machine "speak."

All of these incidents may create negative publicity for our products in the United States. This is more than a hunch. We need to counterattack with positive marketing to prevent a possible reaction from the evangelical consumers in the USA. I am especially sure about this after making my own rice last night. I brought my rice pot to the office. Of course, I have concealed it from all other employees to avoid any misinterpretation. I cannot describe what I've seen here, but I'm sure that you must see it for yourself. Accordingly, I'm requesting that you be at the corporate headquarters at your earliest convenience.

Sincerely,
Yakiko Murota.
Coordinator Customer Care
2 - 8 - 1 2 Minami-Azabu,
Minato, Tokyo 106-0047, Japan
Phone: +81 3-5447-7800
Fax: +81 3-5447-9988

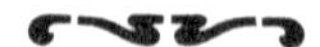

The Doorway

J. P. Lorence

The One picked himself up off the floor on which he had been lying prone. He looked about at the walls around him, and saw in the dim gray light that they were around thirty feet apart. The floor was hard and cold, and the sounds he made echoed deeply, as if the space were far larger than it obviously was.

The One approached the wall in front of him and ran his hands along it. It was a dull, non-reflective surface. There was no sound from within, nothing to indicate an empty space behind. But a sound suddenly did emerge on its own. It was a sound somewhere between a snap and a tear, or more like a dull pop. A crack line of light emerged from the adjacent wall, and part of the surface angled in. It was clearly a door opening.

It swung inward extremely slowly, and the One looked on in trepidation. He quickly realized he didn't know where this place was. He went on to realize he didn't know who *he* was, either. He actually couldn't remember anything at all.

The door opened and revealed the silhouette of another man, somewhat older than the One. He stared blankly for a moment at him, and then approached. The newcomer asked in a quiet voice: "Who are you?"

The One looked at the floor briefly, and then at the sleeves of his shirt, as though his clothing might hold the answer. In fact, it was all the self-description he had at this point. Even his own reflection was unavailable to him. His clothing was casual business attire, a white shirt and black slacks with leather dress shoes.

"I…I can't remember. I just woke up here."

"Then you are the one with no name." He motioned back towards the aperture through which he had just emerged, apparently beckoning the One to follow. "Come, if you wish." The One considered the offer for a moment, and realized that the alternative was remaining in this cold room indefinitely. They both proceeded through the opening. He said hesitantly, "I'm sorry, I don't know what to say…"

"Are you disoriented? Perhaps afraid?"

"Yes. I suddenly found myself here, and I have no idea where this is or anything about it. How did I get here?"

"I don't have all the information you're looking for. This path is a long one. Of course, you must choose it freely and take it as far as you will."

The One listened with a newly found critical ear. Suspicion blossomed where only curiosity had been before. He grasped the newcomer's shoulder and turned him partially around to look in his eyes. *Who was this?*

"Look, don't misunderstand me, but I have no idea who you are or where you've brought me. What is this place about? Do you have any idea how this looks to me? I just found myself in that room in a single moment. Everything is alien."

"How could it be otherwise?" said the newcomer. He glared piercingly down into the One. "Don't you see that this is necessary? Beyond necessary, in fact, it couldn't be otherwise."

"Dammit! I don't need cryptic answers! You have to be straight with me! I had nothing to do with this place, whatever and wherever it is. I just wound up here for no reason I can explain."

"You've just made my point for me, you without a name. As you stated, you popped out of nothing into this situation. Further, you have the audacity to complain because it's unfamiliar. Alien, that was the word. Tell me, how could it be familiar? Since you've just appeared from nothing, you couldn't possibly have played any active part in this place previously. You literally couldn't come into being on any other terms. You would have to find yourself thrown into it, by definition. Is this not so?"

"Yes, I suppose so. Wherever I showed up, this would be the situation, that's what you're saying."

"Quite so. Now that we've settled that, there's somewhere I'd like to take you." The newcomer stopped and pointed upward. He was indicating a square hole in the roof of the hallway with a set of ladder rungs running up one side. "Go that way."

"Are you coming?"

"No. But the answers lie there." With that, he walked on, apparently leaving the choice of which way to go up to the One. He started up the ladder. As he climbed, he thought of what the newcomer had said. And he thought of his fear in the context of it. With every new rung, he could sense the possibility of a fall. But he realized the significance of this, being here meant being here *this* way. His presence had a shape, and it was fearful curiosity.

Up the One climbed. The dull metallic walls glared back sullenly. Finally, after what seemed like thirty yards or more, he saw another opening just ahead. His head cleared it and he looked around. The passage ended with another room. It was smaller than the one he had started in, and a new person occupied it. He climbed in and approached.

This individual was nothing like the first one. It was a teenage girl, perhaps fifteen, huddled in the corner. In front of her lay a rock, a few inches in size, at which she stared blankly. The One asked, "Who are you?" The girl gave no response. "Do you know where we are?" Still no answer.

Finally she stirred slightly. And then she spoke. "We're trapped."

"How did you get here?"

"I don't remember."

"Can you find the way out?"

"There is nothing I can do. I am like this rock," she said.

The One considered the statement for a moment. He wasn't sure what to say, especially with her obvious state. "No, you're not. You can come along and help me find the way out."

"I can do nothing."

The One turned away and searched the walls. The first individual he had met had opened a doorway in the wall somehow. Unless he could find one here, the only other option was returning the way he came.

He started running his hands along the walls to find any deviation in the surface. Then he turned back to the girl and asked, "What is your name?"

"V24."

The designation struck him as strange, but he realized he didn't know his own name, nor could he recall the name of any other person. 'V24' didn't seem like something someone should call herself, but he couldn't say that for certain. "Well, V24, I need to find another way out of this room besides the one I came in. And I can see you won't be much help." V24 went on staring vacantly into the stone in front of her.

"We are nothing. The room is everything."

"You could at least try," he said. V24 gave no further response, and the One went back to searching the walls. He ran his fingers along the textured surface. The grained finish ran along it as far as he could see or feel. Then, suddenly, he saw a break in it. It was a patch about a meter square, and it was polished to a slightly greater reflectivity. He ran his hands along this area as well, and there was no mistaking it. It was something else. The One considered it for a moment, and realized the only thing to do was to push on it. He leaned into the section of the wall.

It remained fixed for a moment, then made the same snapping sound he had heard previously. The square section slid inward about two inches. It stopped, then continued on quickly and was pulled out of sight. The remaining cavity in the wall ran straight ahead as a square tube, big enough for a crawl space. The One looked at it victoriously and returned his gaze to the girl. She seemed to have taken notice of these events slightly, looking vaguely in his direction, although without focus or seeming comprehension.

"See?" said the One. "The rock couldn't have done that. I don't know where it goes, but it's somewhere other than here. And I'm going there, wherever it is."

The young girl named V24 showed a sudden slight spark of what might have been interest or comprehension. She seemed frozen in the moment, as though the realization had stuck her in time. But the moment faded from her countenance, and her head slowly returned to the rock. Her gaze seemed to sink down to it, as though her eyes were marbles rolling downhill, and the lowest point was looking straight at the stone before her. She made no further movement or sound.

The One felt as though he should do something, but short of physically dragging her, which would be impossible given the size of the passage, he could see no remaining options. Clearly, whoever she was, she had decided to stay here. As for himself, he would have to continue for the time being.

Without saying another word, he took to the tunnel and went forward. It was a perfectly square, blank crawl space, just large enough for one person to fit through. It seemed to go on for a good distance, but he could see the end of it. After maybe five minutes, he was there, and out the One climbed into yet another room.

This one was quite small. It had another crawl space, identical to the one he had just emerged from, at the opposite end. In one corner lay a book. It was a small leather-bound volume, with no marking on the cover. He opened it and started reading.

The subject awoke in a blank room with no previous memory. He searched about along the walls. A sound came from behind one of the walls, and a doorway opened from one wall of the room. Another subject joined him and the two began to converse. The first subject asked...

The One slammed the book shut. It was an obvious record of the events he had just experienced. How was this possible? Had someone been following him and recording the circumstances? If so, how did they get ahead of him to leave the book? And aside from that, it was printed text. That might be possible if it were handwritten, but a printed page must have been made in advance. And here it was. He flipped forward to see where the description went. After about twenty-five pages, the text ran out, and he went back a few to see how it ended. "This is right about where I should be at..."

The subject moved on from the room containing the previous model. He followed the passage forward, and knew this way was forward thanks to his previous encounter with the static version. The memory of the encounter drove him onward. He was determined to find the way out, and encountered the log along the way. As he began reading...

"Now I'm reading about myself reading." The One closed the book again. He dwelled a moment on what he had just been told about his own position here. He didn't want to end up like the girl who called herself V24, and he and the book in front of him both knew that.

He closed the book to look at the cover. It was blank, and he looked at the back. It had the word "Log" written on it upside down, near the bottom. No, wait, this was the front, and the word was right side up! He'd been reading from the back!

"Well, that doesn't make any sense! Why was it printed to read from back to front?" The One set the book down and decided to continue through the next passage. As he did, he couldn't help but keep thinking of the volume he had just found. How did it know how he felt as he tried to escape this place? And what was it really trying to say?

The One groped along the passage. There must be some escape from this place. It was clearly some sort of prison. What might lie ahead? Danger? A dead end? Might it loop back? That last possibility was inconceivably terrifying. He had to try, and this direction was his only hope.

The memory of the encounter drove him onward. This sentence kept coming back to mind. Then suddenly, he stopped dead in his tracks.

"Wait! That's why it was at the back! Now I get it!" The passage was only seen by him as an escape because of what he had just seen. It wasn't just his memory; it was his sense of direction too. "The past rides in front. I lead with it. That's why the book is backwards."

The One saw the end of the passage. It terminated with a door bordered by a seal of some sort. Clearly it opened outward. In the center of the door was a hand wheel about ten inches in diameter. Could this be it?

"I don't know what lies out there. But I know what lies in here, and that's all that matters." The One committed himself and turned with all his strength at the wheel. With great resistance, it began to open. The seal cracked, and a sucking sound came from the opening. The One realized it was a vacuum on the other side. He stopped for a moment, and the hissing continued as he thought. He looked behind himself and looked back at the door. The One seized the wheel and turned it fiercely. The latch released completely and the door flung open, pulling the One out of the passage with incredible force. He looked straight ahead and reached out his arms to embrace…nothing.

"Vaal…Vaal, wake up! Are you all right?" A faded picture of a young woman crystallized, and the distorted sound of her voice suddenly resonated into familiarity even after it was silent. The One looked at his own hands, the padded platform he was lying on, and the vidcom twisted on its flex pole, angled awkwardly above his head. On the screen he read the first line: *Mitzri Vaal, Unit 312.* On seeing his own name, his identity returned completely, and he felt for the halo strapped to his forehead. "Dammit, get this thing off me Kanli!"

"Hold on Vaal, I've got you." Danyl Kanli reached behind his head and separated the Velcro strap, pulling the halo's contacts off his forehead. Two red circles stood out where the contacts had made the read / write surface.

Mitzri Vaal, software engineer, fourth class, sat up in his bed and took stock of the situation. Why was no psychmedic present? Of course, his HR liaison, Kanli, was here, but that was a given. "Kanli, why did you pull me out? I was almost at the end of the tape."

"You *were* at the end of the tape. Your ENC looked shaky towards the end, and I thought of pulling the safety a couple of times, but I guessed you were making progress. It ran to the end of the recording and the frame booted you out, just as it should have."

"Thanks for letting it run. Those last two minutes were crucial. I was stuck in a passage…"

Just then, a medic walked in "I got a call. Session's finished? Any problems waking up?"

"No, I'm fine. I'd like a typepad if you have one handy."

"I'll see if I can find one. If you didn't know, there's a voice recorder on the vid over your head. But get some rest. I'll come back with a pad as soon as I can find one."

"Wonderful." Vaal looked at Kanli's concerned expression and said, "Thanks for keeping watch. I'll have a report for human resources in the morning. I might need to rest a bit for now."

"I'll see you tomorrow. Message me if you want to talk," came her reply.

Vaal was about to tell her he would, but the words died on his lips. He was unconscious before they left the room.

The vidcom hummed slightly and felt warm to the touch, as they always did, and Vaal levered it into position above his desk. "Emerge touchscreen," he said. The blue tone of the screen vanished and was replaced by a set of circles indicating function triggers. He accessed his log file of the previous day's events which he had composed in the morning. "Copy to Conference Room Seventeen." he commanded the operating system.

Even as he did it, a voice came over the vid. It was one of the secretaries. "Eng Mitzri, they're waiting for you in C17."

"I know. I'm on my way. Thank you."

The door slid open sideways and silently, and Vaal looked at an all too familiar scene. Six individuals in grey jumpsuits sat around a semicircular table. The group themselves ranged in age from about twenty-five to sixty, from what could be seen. *That young one must be quite a prodigy to be in with this gang.* Vaal thought to himself.

These were second class Data Theorists, information architects who had worked their way up the IT industry's corporate ladder. Their alleged function was system development, but the real point of their work was to find the answers to the deepest questions that information science

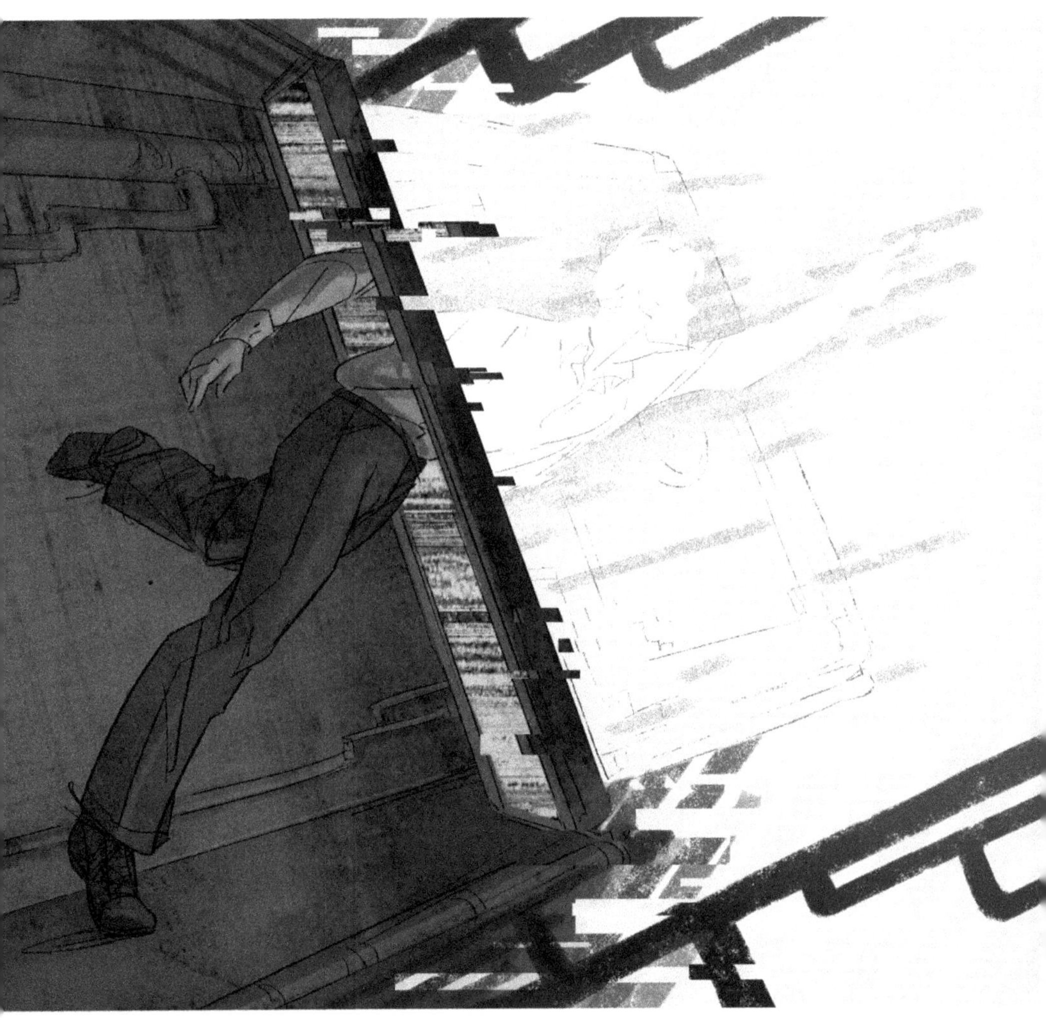

raised. The topic had once been called Philosophy of Information Science. Now it was more modestly termed Data Theory. True to their calling, these people were here to interview the Data Engineer who had read the tape of their current project, and who hopefully had the answers to the questions of why it was stalled. Mitzri Vaal took the center of the room and addressed his audience.

"Thank you for coming. As I'm sure you already know, my name is Eng Mitzri, fourth class, and I'm here to report on the Synthetic Sentience Project which our division has been handling for the last seven months. I was recently promoted to acting lead of the project, and as such, it was left up to me to review the tape of our current version's test run. My report on the session is in the conference room's inbox, should you wish to copy it."

The entire group seemed to shift with obvious discomfort. Finally, one of the group, a middle aged, soft-spoken man with piercing eyes, did so. "As a matter of fact, Eng Mitzri, we skimmed your report while you were on your way up here. We were rather curious as to why your psyche interpreted the tape that way. You must admit, it was rather…novel."

Vaal looked at him for a moment, trying to guess why the man looked familiar. With a sudden burst of recognition he drew the connection. *That was the first person I met in the dream! He dubbed me "the one with no name!"*

He shrugged off the impression and continued. "As you probably know, we developed several prototype versions of the software and tried to get them to perform tasks that would reveal self-awareness. These tests eventually took the form of building a frame for it to run inside, one that specifically had no clear entrance or exit points. The software would simply start running inside the frame and have to find its own way out. If it could do this, we guessed, it would be demonstrable that it was issuing itself commands, and not simply responding to its own code syntax. After failing to even activate the first several inside the frame, and then seeing Version Twenty-Four get stuck in a software loop, we constructed Version Twenty-Five and let it run."

The oldest member of the group, a grey-haired woman, broke in. "Yes, I was briefed on that. I was under the impression it spontaneously decompiled when it reached the exterior of the frame."

"Our team was under the same impression at first. But the signature on the tape didn't indicate the residue that such an event would have produced. So I volunteered to do a virtual review of the recording of the software's process of escaping the frame. Mediated, of course, in terms my unconscious would understand."

The young man commented: "Quite a colorful unconscious you must have, too, Eng Mitzri. I wish my dreams were this good. Metal tunnels, catatonic teenage girls, why, I might have to try that tape out myself."

"You should, I strongly recommend it." Vaal retorted. Silently, he thought to himself: *It would take that imbecile grin off your face for some time.*

"So what conclusion did you come to out of the virtual experience?" asked the one in the middle. "What happened to our software?"

"I'm coming to that. In the course of my journey through its path of development, I encountered the same issues it faced discovering the nature of its existence. It's not an easy matter to escape from a virtual frame with no prior memory or sense of place, I can tell you. The greatest issue that struck me along the way was the encounter with Version Twenty Four, which appeared to me as a young girl. I had to make a choice at every step along the way, and that element became clear when I met her. I pressed on, and she gave up."

"No!" interjected the young one again. "V24 is looped. It had an internal failure due to a design flaw."

"Call it that if you wish, but there's more to the story. Remember, this is a *sentience* project. The software is really making choices, not just responding to commands, assuming it is actually functioning. I looked into V24's eyes, she knew what was happening and acknowledged the situation, yet she just sat there. This brings us to my major discovery, and this one will be right up your alley. *The software has to choose to survive.*"

The last comment made a clear impact on the entire team. The implications of it were obvious. The one in the middle spoke up again. "So the flaw can't be engineered out? Is that your claim?"

"I wouldn't put it that way. I would say that if you try to design out the option of freezing, as V24 did, you miss the point of the project. It has to be able to choose, and that's a choice it can always make. What could be done is, give it the tools it needs to survive, build it a frame it can reasonably mature from, and make continuously redeveloped models until you find the personality you want. Eventually you'll find the version of the software you're looking for, and it will live on its own terms."

They sat silent for a long moment, apparently absorbing the message. Finally, the old woman spoke up. "Well, I believe that's all we need from you, Eng Mitzri. Thank you for your time, and especially for your candid answers." They all rose to leave. Vaal watched them exit the room one after another, looks of deep concern on their faces.

The young one was the last to exit. Just before he did, he turned to look at Vaal, a look of puzzlement on his face. "I need to ask you something. I jumped ahead to the end of your report. When you were at the airlock and you jumped through it, were you trying to kill yourself? I mean, I know it's just a tape, and it's for the software that I'm asking, I really want to know if decomposition is an issue at the edge of the framework. But that said, did you think you would die?"

Vaal paused awkwardly before answering. "As I remember it, I had the impression that a vacuum was better than a hole. So I left." The D-Theorist let a flicker of comprehension cross his countenance, and left the room to join the others.

Mitzri Vaal sank into his office chair and stared at the ceiling. He was emotionally exhausted from the events of the last two days. The vid flickered to life. *Message from Danyl Kanli.* He opened it.

"Call me when you get in, Vaal. I want to hear how the meeting went."

He opened the channel to her desk and she appeared on the vid. "So, how did it go? Did you blow them away?"

"Like a puff of smoke. You know how easily impressed the firm's D-Theory department is."

Kanli only laughed in response. "So when are you coming over for dinner like you promised? Jax has been asking about you. He took quite a liking to you last time."

"Tell him soon. I'd love to visit you both, but I'll need a few days off after this episode. Believe it or not, I'm still having flashes from the tape review."

Her expression suddenly became serious, as this was a matter for her department to manage. But after a moment, it softened, and she said, "Take a few days if you need them. Call me from home if you need anything."

"Count on it, Kanli. And tell Jax I said hi."

"I will. Oh, and by the way, take the Tube home, don't drive. The news just covered a major accident on Interzone Nine."

"Thanks for the tip. I'll talk to you later." He switched the vid to Zone News and selected the traffic report. A skycam was doing close-ups of the vehicles stranded in the jam. The news reporter's voice overlaid the images, saying, "All this caused by one overturned freighter in a middle lane! The whole IZ is shut down for almost twelve kilometers! Let's get a close-up of a few of these drives and see how the motorists are doing!"

The camera zoomed in on one expensive looking newer drive, slightly crooked in the lane, its window rolled down. The occupant appeared nearly forty, and was obviously shouting at the dashboard vid, on which could be seen the image of another person with whom he was presumably conferencing. The driver smacked the steering wheel and spat out his window in disgust before leaning back and putting his hands over his face.

Vaal watched the entire display stone-faced up to the last moment, then burst out laughing explosively. All he could say was, "Good luck, V24!"

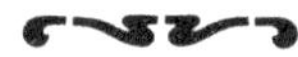

Monkey Business

M. P. Diederich

"**W**elcome to the monkey house," says Dr. Jules, grinning so widely that the skin at both corners of his mouth accordions together in a stunning latticework of canyons and wrinkles. Lex attempts to laugh, nervously tucks her hair behind her ears.

"Of course, these are chimps, not monkeys," Dr. Jules continues, gesturing toward the mass of apes beyond the reinforced glass partition. Lex watches one of the chimps squatting near the wall as it thumbs through the pages of a tattered issue of *National Geographic*, pausing every once in a while to tear out a page and stuff it into its mouth. "They're mostly females now, but Dr. Involuntario's hoping our recent progress will convince the board to increase our male population."

Lex nods, unsure of whether to ask what sort of progress has been made, or what male chimpanzees have to do with anything. Instead, she stares at the apes swinging around on artificial branches or picking at each other's fur. One of the males scratches his anus and chews on his paw.

"So, um, what exactly are you doing with all of them?" Lex asks.

"Living," says Dr. Jules. "Can't you tell? Each day that passes without one of them dropping dead is considered a success."

He attempts another wide smile, but again it just comes off as a Gwynplaine rictus grin. Lex turns away, back to the apes.

"It's slightly more complicated than that," says Dr. Jules. "We'd probably be better served starting from the beginning. This way."

They walk down the long, clean white corridor to a small, dim room filled with several massive aquaria. After Lex's eyes begin to adjust to the darkness, she begins to make out small shapes darting around inside the aquaria. Mice? No.

"Yes, cockroaches," says Dr. Jules, again beaming that hideous smile. You'd think a good-looking man like him would learn to smile like a normal person by his age. "These are all specially bred, of course. Didn't want to leave anything to chance. Each one has a tiny computer implanted in place of its brain. What you're looking at here is the world's first colony of fully functioning, cybernetic organisms."

Lex forces herself to peer closely at the mass of oversized insects scurrying about inside the aquarium. Apart from the one crawling in circles on the side of the tank, nothing about them seems out of the ordinary. Is he putting her on?

"I know. It doesn't look like much, but there was a good thirty years of research spent just getting us to this point. You see, even the simplest macroscopic animals require a complex configuration of nerves and neuroarchitecture in order to function normally. Roaches were the easiest first step, since they can live for days without their heads."

"Then how do you know that the computers in their heads work?"

"Well, many of these roaches have been alive for quite some time—years in some cases, which accounts for their large size. The computers fully replace their brains, which means that if they're capable of feeding themselves and avoiding danger long enough to survive, then the artificial brains we designed for them must be doing the job, right?"

"I suppose so?"

"Here," he says. "Watch this." He walks over to a computer terminal next to the aquarium and enters a short series of commands. All of the roaches in the aquarium suddenly freeze, then quickly scurry into a perfect square formation in the center of the tank. Dr. Jules chuckles softly. "Now watch this," he says, typing another command. The roaches scurry into a smiley face formation, captioned with the words *Hello Lex McGreevey.*

"Wow," says Lex. "Hello roaches."

"Remarkable, isn't it?" says Dr. Jules. "Yes, we had quite a bit of fun with the roach commands. In the early days we used to have them fight each other—I mean actually get up on their hind legs and throw punches. We'd place bets on them, have weigh-ins. It's amazing what you can do with a zombie roach."

"So, you just sit around playing with bugs all day?"

"Not at all. You see, it was all part of the process of creating a functional cybernetic being. We had to start small, engineering simple creatures so we could insert a readymade computer to handle the majority of the work for us. What came next was the really hard part."

Dr. Jules presses a succession of keys on the terminal and the roaches go back to their aimless scurrying. Lex follows the scientist and his disturbing grin down the hallway to the next room, this one much more brightly lit. The room contains a row of three cages, each containing a single white mouse.

"When we mastered the art of cyborg insects, we felt it was time to take the leap into true vivisection. This required a more complex nervous system, and so we moved on to laboratory mice bred for extremely low intelligence. Borderline retardation, in fact."

Lex leans in for a close look at one of the perfectly normal-seeming mice, watches it run around a bit in its wheel. One of the others roots around in the wood shavings covering the bottom of its cage. Retarded?

"I've worked with a lot of lab mice," says Lex. "These guys seem all right to me."

"Well, that's the idea," says Dr. Jules. "Each of the mice in these cages is fitted with an artificial hippocampus, as well as a few minor alterations to the cerebral cortex. We then use a wireless connection to feed information into the mouse's brain—basic hunting techniques, maps of mazes, minor problem-solving methods. What's been most remarkable is how well the surviving mice have managed to retain all this new information. It was a real breakthrough."

"The surviving mice?" asks Lex.

"Well, we had an initial failure rate of about 68%, which increased as time went on. The reconstruction of a being's central nervous system isn't exactly easy; most of the mice never even woke up. These three here are the only ones who lived."

"But you didn't alter the procedure, even just to see if you could improve the survivability?"

"Why bother? They're just mice. We proved that Dr. Involuntario's basic concept was possible, and that we could continue to proceed along those lines. That's where the dogs come in. This way, please."

And now back out into the blinding light of the corridor and across, through soundproof doors and into a cacophony of snarls and barks and yips. A miasma of dog flesh, matted fur and feces. Man's best friend indeed, Lex thinks.

"Now, most of the canines here are the failed subjects. The more successful ones are in another facility out in Rahway where they can be much more comfortable. These dogs here have exhibited deep behavioral issues, though nothing out of the realm of statistical averages—especially considering the nature of the experiments. You see, we used a similar

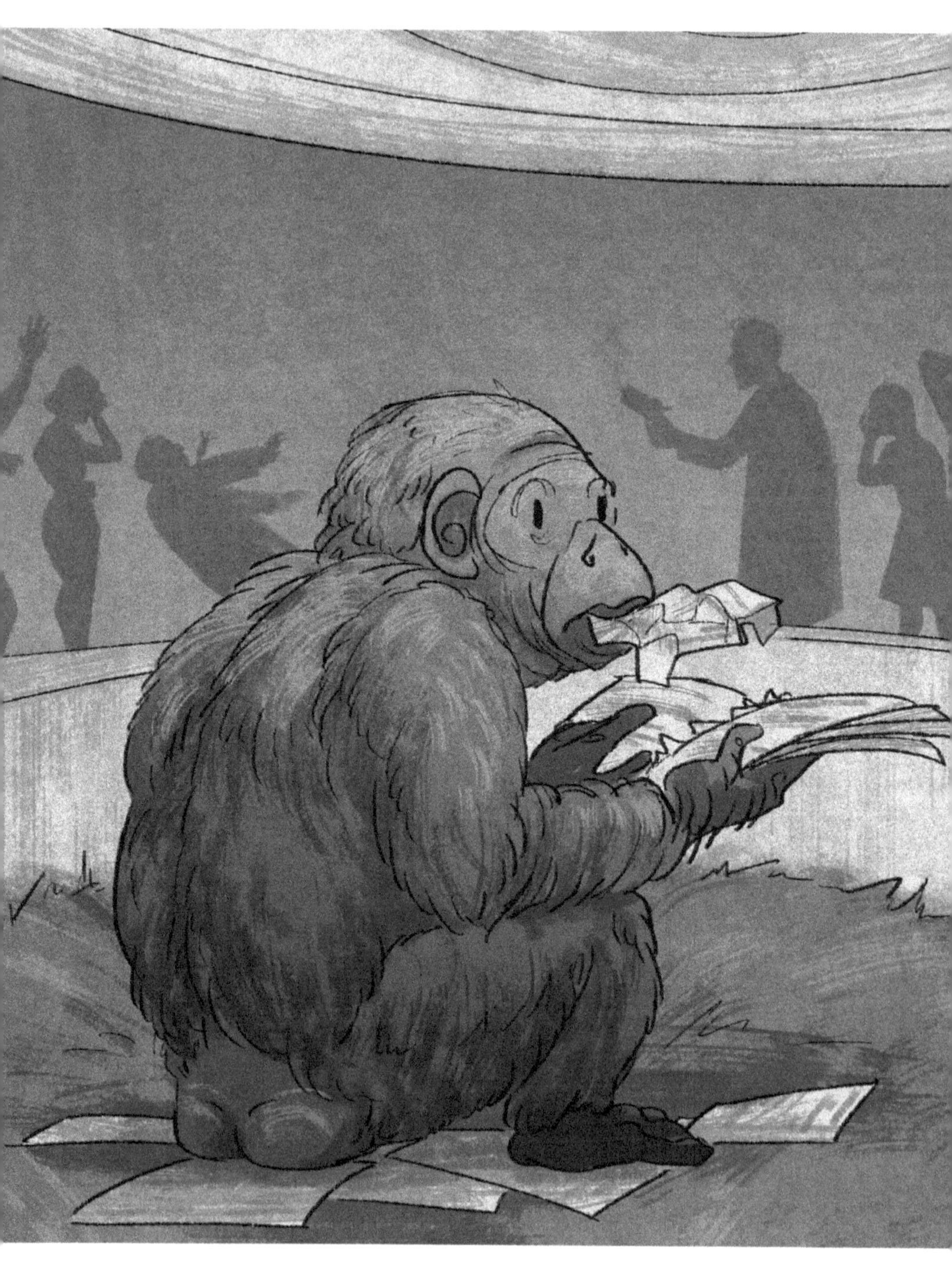

device to the one we used for the mice, though with the dogs we left most of the basic brain architecture intact. The device was specifically wired to the optic and olfactory nerves in each of the dogs, allowing us to transmit various stimuli. At first the stimuli were all simple—say, the image of a raw steak and the scent of garbage. First, we'd transmit the visual of the steak and the smell of the steak directly to the dog's brain, then gauge its reaction."

"I'm sorry," says Lex, "but how do you transmit the smell of a steak?"

"Quite simple," says Dr. Jules. "We hooked up EEG sensors to the dogs, then presented them with various smells, sights, sensations, etc. We recorded the brain activity involved with each reaction, which allowed us to then calibrate the device to target specific parts of the dogs' brains in order to duplicate the various stimuli. It took a while, but that's why you have interns."

"Wow."

"Indeed. Now where was I? Ah yes. So, we'd gauge the dogs' reaction to the artificial steak. Normally this resulted in a state of confusion for the dog, since they could see and smell the steak, but when they bit at where it appeared to be, they found only air. They'd even start to salivate prodigiously."

"But…why? I mean, it's remarkable to accomplish all this, but why did you need to make digital steaks for dogs?"

"Well, that was the basic tool we needed to advance to the next phase of the experiment. Obviously, if the dog sees and smells a steak, it believes a steak is present. We just wanted to establish that our technology was effective in this regard. After the initial round, we began a new experiment in which we would display the virtual steak, but then transmit the smell of cooked carrots. For the majority of the dogs, this still triggered salivation, but they appeared somewhat anxious about the incongruity of the sight and the smell. We alternated the images and the smells, until the dogs ultimately fell into two distinct groups."

"Those being…?"

"The first group—the ones that recognized the difference between the instances of matching stimuli and the disparate ones—these dogs were subjected to an even more complicated test in which we created a sort of Pavlovian reward system. The dogs were given various visual stimuli, such as a cat, or a toy, or a bowl of food; sometimes the smells corresponded to the image, sometimes they did not. We then rewarded them for reacting to the images that displayed with smells that didn't correspond. The results were rather remarkable."

"What did it prove, though? That you can mess up a dog's sense of reality?"

"Well, in some cases, that was the result, yes. Most of the dogs you see here have started to display brain function patterns normally found only in schizophrenic humans. They respond to most stimuli with anger and hostility. The successful subjects, however, demonstrated a rather incredible ability to differentiate between symbolic objects and real ones. Even more remarkably, the successful subjects were conditioned to react to the symbolic objects in order to receive a reward. It's not perfect, but it's an incredible step toward the understanding of basic symbolic communication. The implications here…well, I may be getting ahead of myself."

"This is all really fascinating," says Lex, "but what about the chimps?"

"Well, that's the truly fascinating part," says Dr. Jules, rubbing his palms together as yet another horrible rictus grin stretches across his face. "You see—"

"You can see she has no idea what you're talking about," says a tall man in a tattered lab coat, leaning against the wall of the corridor.

"Ah, I didn't realize you were there, sir," says Dr. Jules. "Ms. Lex McGreevey, I'd like you to meet Dr. Efecto Involuntario, the head of the Advatech Research Division."

"I've read so much about your work," says Lex. "I didn't realize you were so young."

"You were probably reading about my father," says Involuntario. "Everyone gets us confused, you know."

"I was just showing Lex around the lab here," says Dr. Jules. "She's going to be working as, um, well, the replacement lab assistant."

"Yes, someone has to euthanize the mice," says Involuntario. "She'll learn what she needs to know as we go along, Verne."

"Yes, of course," says Dr. Jules. "I just thought that, since this is more of a bookkeeping day and all…"

"Yes, I know, you thought you'd impress the new assistant with a whole explanation of our lab work here. That's not the way things are done here, Verne. No offense, Ms. McGreevey, but we have to maintain a tight level of security about these projects of ours. Patent pending and all that, yes?"

"Oh, absolutely," says Lex. "I understand."

"Very good," says Involuntario. "Now, Verne, if you'll show Ms. McGreevey to the mice she'll be…dispatching?"

"Ah, yes," says Dr. Jules. "Right this way, Lex."

"It's an honor to meet you, Dr. Involuntario," says Lex, back over her shoulder as she follows Dr. Jules down the hall. Involuntario acknowledges her with a nod. They get younger all the time, and here he is as the grand old man of the laboratory, just as his father had been before him. My god, how many years had it been since…

Now a sudden whoosh! The elevator door opens and a group of seven suited figures emerges, led by Dalton Falcomaltes, Casper Mimesis, and a silver-haired woman of about 60 whom Involuntario vaguely recognizes.

"…and this is, of course, our, er, top secret research facility. Originally this was the Arcadia Steel company's private fallout shelter. Designed to withstand a 40 Megaton blast, if I'm not mistaken?"

"I believe that was kilotons, sir," Mimesis corrects.

"Yes, er, um, right. Anyway, yes. This is our top-level research laboratory, headed up by Dr. Involuntario, who just so happens to be right here to meet us. Good morning, Efecto."

"Good morning, Dalton."

"Efecto, I'd like you to meet Ms. Eloise St. John-Featherstonehaugh," says Falcomaltes, smiling proudly at having pronounced the CEO's name correctly. "She's the head of Zeitgeist and, by extension, Advatech."

"Pleasure to meet you," says Involuntario.

"The pleasure is all mine, Doctor," says ESJF, making a point of not looking at Involuntario's stained, tattered lab coat. "I'm very familiar with your father's work, as well as your own advancements these later years. This is quite a facility you have down here."

"Yes, we, er, haven't spared you any expense, eh, Efecto?"

"I want more chimps," says Involuntario.

"Haha, yes, well, er, we'll discuss that at a, um, later date then, eh?" Falcomaltes forces our a laugh. "Why don't you show us around your laboratory then, Efecto?"

"Well, you've caught us on a bookkeeping day. Lots of sweeping out the dead or dying animals. Would you like to hear about our progress with the chimpanzees?"

"Oh, absolutely!" Falcomaltes chirps. "Come this way, everyone."

"Excuse me for asking," says ESJF, "but I happened to glance through the window there and noticed a man strapped to the bed."

"Oh him? That's part of a sleep-research study we've been working on. Had some strange results with it, actually."

"Strange how?"

"Well, that man's been asleep for eight days."

"Isn't that considered a coma?"

"Normally, yes. But in this particular case the brain activity has been quite…DALTON! I wouldn't go in there if I were you."

"Oh? I, er, thought we might show Ms, er, St. John the monkeys."

"Chimps, Dalton. And trust me—it's much safer through the viewing glass."

"Well, always, er, do as the doctor orders, eh?"

"And you said you wanted more chimpanzees, Dr. Involuntario?" asks ESJF. "There seem to be quite a large number in there already."

"Ah—well, you, er, see, um, Ms. St. John-Featherstonehaugh, Dr. Involuntario is attempting to alter the brain functions of a large population in order to see what sorts of potential issues might arise from a large-scale implementation of this, er, technology. The monkeys—"

"Chimpanzees."

"Yes, right. Er, chimpanzees. Well, they are really the best test subjects for this sort of high-level cognitive work. With their relatively superior brain function, they're really the only animals capable of understanding any level of symbolic representation. Do I have that right, Efecto?"

"No."

"I hate to interrupt, gentlemen, but I'm still not entirely clear on what Dr. Involuntario is trying to accomplish down here," says St. John-Featherstonehaugh.

"Well, er, for the past twenty years, Advatech has been hard at work pioneering the next frontier in neuro-enhancement. What Dr. Involuntario is attempting to create here is a device with fully wireless connectivity and transmission abilities. We're already researching the marketing possibilities for this device."

"This would be the Enhancemitter you spoke of earlier?" asks Hans Wudtenschaftler, Zeitgeist's VP of Medical Products.

"You told them about it already?" Involuntario asks Falcomaltes.

"Er, yes. I didn't see any harm in it. You're, haha, almost done with testing, right, Efecto?"

"Certainly not. Just the other day my old lab assistant was attacked by one of the test subjects. They're not responding as well as I would have hoped."

"Efecto, can we discuss all this later? I, er…"

"Have you even seen what these creatures can do to a man? They're absolutely brutal. They go straight for your eyes, hands, and genitals. Hell, the poor son of a bitch lost his—"

"Wait a minute, Efecto. I—"

"Gentlemen, may I interrupt you again for a moment?" asks St. John-Featherstonehaugh.

"How do you expect me to justify the purchase of even more male chimpanzees if you can't even keep the ones you have from maiming your assistants?" asks Falcomaltes.

"Maiming?" asks Wudtenschaftler.

"They only attack other male animals," says Involuntario. "That's why they tore off Jacob's—"

"Gentlemen! If I may…"

"I'm terribly sorry, Ms. S. You were saying?"

"Dr. Involuntario, I would really appreciate if you would explain what exactly it is that your department is up to with this…well, this little zoo you have set up down here."

"The chimpanzees specifically? Or do you mean the cockroaches and the dogs and the mice and everything?"

"All of it, Efecto. She means all of it."

"Well, that's really more of Dr. Jules's department, Ms. St. John-Featherstonehaugh. I really deal with the chimpanzees more directly these days. They're far more vital to the entire project. We've recently fitted all of them with a basic neural transmitter-receiver. It connects directly with their optic nerve, as well as several other important areas of the brain. We've been running some rudimentary exercises with them, having them interact with a basic virtual display projecting in their field of vision. Results so far have been…well, mixed."

"Mixed, Dr. Involuntario?"

"I believe he means that this is all part of the scientific process, Ms, er, St. John-Featherstonehaugh. It's really—"

"I wasn't speaking to you, Dalton. And just call me Eloise if you can't pronounce my name correctly. You were saying, Dr. Involuntario?"

"Well, the test subjects are having a difficult time with the essential functioning of the virtual interface. They become confused about the idea of objects appearing before them which aren't actually there. They become quite hostile, actually."

"I see. Is there a solution to this problem?"

"We want to make some alterations to the interface program before we come to any definite conclusions about the basic concept of the technology. The hardware, as far as we can tell, is working perfectly. The software's the sticking point right now."

"Quite. And what, may I ask, is the overall goal here?"

"If I may, er, explain, Ms. St…er, Eloise. The goal with this series of experiments is to determine the feasibility of augmenting the human brain with a device that allows for direct Internet access in the brain. Imagine, if you will, a, er, human brain with a constant link to all the information it could ever need—and instantly accessible. This would, of course, be a momentous development for the Millennium Project."

"I thought we weren't calling it that anymore," says Involuntario.

"Well, er, for lack of a better term…"

"If you don't mind my saying so, gentlemen, this all sounds like a lot of research for the sake of research. I mean, Internet connectivity is all well and good, but it seems like a lot of work just to develop a web browser."

"Well, that, er, is the, um, starting point, Ms…um, Eloise. Efecto's hope—mine as well, mind you—is that this new device will allow for all sorts of new advancements in the treatment of mental illnesses like schizophrenia and depression—even autism. The possibilities are quite, er, breathtaking."

"But it's all still theoretical," says Involuntario.

"Well, er, yes and no, he means. I'm sure Dr. Lapham can elaborate on the considerable gains he's making in the use of electrode therapy with some of the clinical depressives under his care?"

All eyes turn to Lapham, standing off to the side of the group.

"Well, that's all still up in the air," he says, smoothing his gray hair. "It's rather crude, what Dr. Branchwater's doing up at Haven. At least, when compared to all of this. We're poking around in the dark, really."

"What I'd really like is to see whether we can, er, get to early stage human testing on this device," says Falcomaltes. "I know it's still early, but if there's a way to start gauging the psychotherapeutic aspects of the Enhancemitter, surely it's not something we can really test on the monkeys."

"Chimpanzees."

"Er, right."

"I'm not sure Branchwater's gonna like that idea at all," says Lapham.

"And neither do I!" cries Hans Wudtenschaftler. "Replacing medication with computers? What the hell are you trying to do, kill the pharmaceutical wing of the company?"

"Now, see here, Hans—no one's trying to—"

"Oh, no one's ever trying to do anything. You're just going ahead and tossing out decades of confirmed pharmaceutical research. Not to mention all our demonstrated results. To think that after all these years…"

"Hans, I think you're, um, er, overreacting quite a bit here."

"Like hell I am! You all just can't wait to start having cyborgs running around with electronic brains, to the point that you're all here debating how to screw up the psychotropics wing of the pharma industry. I'm of half a mind to—GAAH!"

With a loud thud, Wudtenschaftler's considerable mass falls to the floor, a large red dart protruding from his neck. Dr. Involuntario slides his tranquilizer gun back into his lab coat pocket.

"You'll all have to excuse me," he says. "I have a lot of work to do."

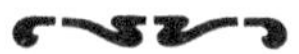

The Dead and Eternal

Rob Hartzell

In the Cloud, the dead are never entirely dead; they can never truly be gone as long as a backup of them remains intact. They may lose time—a week, a month, a year or more in the rarest cases—but all the engineers have to do is hit the restore button and there they are again, almost exactly the way you remember them. *Almost*: that's the tricky part; they fit so comfortably into the old routine, a *them*-shaped hole they'd left in you, that you can easily forget there's a blank spot in their memories—a hole in them (as you so recently knew them) where *you* used to fit. Try as you might, you can never recreate that lost time, especially if it goes beyond a week; you can tell them about it, but that usually leads to awkwardness, no matter how gamely they try to jump back into the role. Things are never the same. Those who have been restored cannot always be totally restored.

Soleil has fallen in love with me in three iterations out of the five she's had. You would think that I might get used to the process of mourning and restoration, but I haven't. I don't think I ever will. There is no word for the grief that remains when the one you've loved and lost is only partly restored to you. The closest might be shame, which at least gets at what it feels like to mourn someone that—at some essential level—is not really gone. On the one hand, I take a certain amount of comfort— however qualified and severely limited—that I appear to get the benefit of the doubt 60% of the time. On the other hand, I find myself wondering if I deserve to be that lucky, that much loved.

The first time Soleil had to be restored, she'd become infected with a bit of malware that shut her down cold in mid-sentence. We had been talking about something perfectly inconsequential—gossiping about the engineers who were supposed to watch over us and protect us from exactly these sorts of things, maybe, something like that. We had been together for a little less than a month, which also happened to be the virus' incubation period. I had thought there was a burp in the network at first; when she didn't reconnect, I started to ping her network address frantically to make sure the line was still there. When the engineers told me what happened, I felt…*queasy* isn't the right word for someone without a body, but that dazed, sick feeling crosses the silicon barrier. I pulled up her social media profiles repeatedly, re-read her posts for hours on end until I'd almost memorized them.

When she came back online, her memories of the two of us stopped before we had become a proper couple—an Us, a We. I don't honestly know what she'd been told about that time. She never even tried to make contact with me. I tried to let go of her, though I couldn't help sneaking a peek at her status updates every now and again. I watched and hoped that she might change her mind about that much. She never got a chance: she was reinfected with the same virus, and had to be restored again—and witnessing it a second time, from a distance, was no easier than it was the first time around, up close.

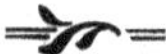

Soleil[3] saw my grief—*I could feel it palpably, as if we still had flesh to touch it with,* she told me once—and took pity on me. Can I say that I have loved one iteration of her above another? I had more time with Soleil[3] than with the original; maybe that's what colors my memory of her. Or maybe it's the way she let me grieve her original upload, even though the Soleil I was talking to was just as authentically her as that "original" had been. *She wouldn't want you to suffer alone; I know this much.* It took most of a year before I could get past the loss of Soleil[1] and the subsequent iterations that followed…and even when I did stop mourning, it wasn't like it was before. We weren't what we were before—how could we be?—but what we did have was good; maybe even better than before. We grew in-jokes between us. We got each other's obscure references. She understood me more deeply than anyone has, pre- or post-upload, maybe even more than I do. And at one time, I understood her, or thought I did. Two iterations since then, I'm even less sure than I ever was…

Soleil[3] and I had three years together before an electromagnetic pulse attack at her server-compound erased her and her onsite backups

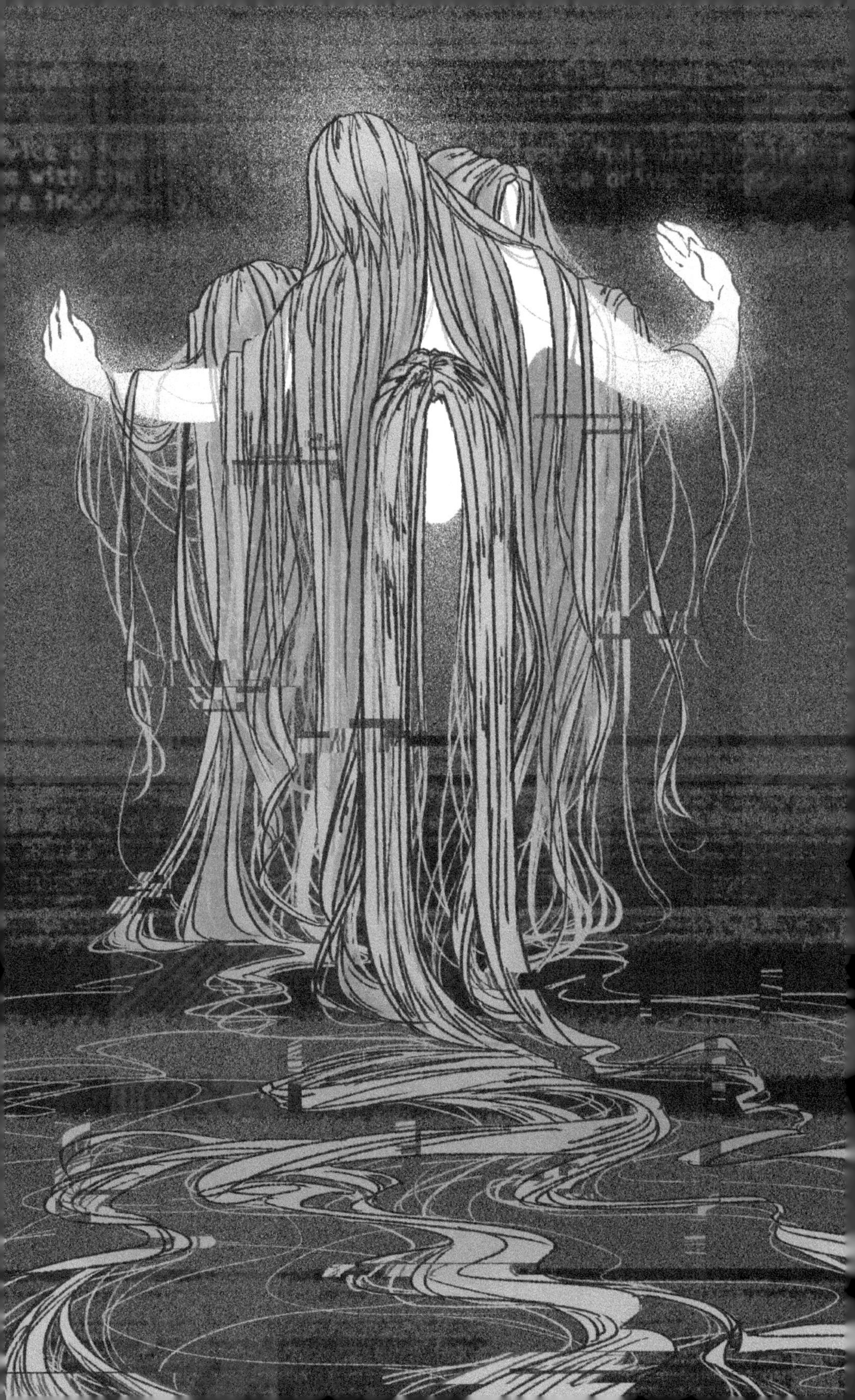

completely. Soleil[4] had to be reinstated from the same backup Soleil[3] had respawned from, and she was uncomfortable with the idea of having me as a friend once I'd told her (or tried to) what we'd been before. And I could scarcely blame her; by then, having already lost four iterations/incarnations of Soleil, I was too far-gone with grief to deal with yet another iteration. I left her alone, though I did, admittedly, peer in on her status updates to see how she was doing—I wanted her to be well, even if she didn't want to be "with" me, I begged the engineers to reset me from a backup—to let me forget what I've lost, if only so I can truly regain it—but they wouldn't do it. Some nonsense about ethical and legal grey areas and the sanctity of consciousness, et cetera…

Every now and again, I found myself wondering if enough time had passed, if it would be worth it to break the ice, no matter what happened or where it went from there. I never got any further than that though; by the time I'd screwed the nerve up to do something, she'd already been restored yet again, for reasons which are still a mystery to me. Soleil[5] has never mentioned it, and if nothing else, after all this time, I've learned not to ask…

If Soleil[3] was the love of my life, Soleil[5] is the Grand Passion. The knowledge of her four deaths has made her almost completely uninhibited. She weaves back and forth between French and English whenever we talk—especially when we're in the SexBox together. Her laugh, in those moments, is an echo of a belly laugh across time, and the wires that connect us, alike. Her love—our love—is feral: all *stürm-und-drang, liebe-und-krieg*; she is angry with me now because I noticed that she swears in English most of the time, something I haven't seen since Soleil[2]. *You will never truly love me*, she tells me, *you will never truly live in the moment, if you keep harkening back to these earlier Soleils. How am I supposed to live knowing that you're comparing me to old ghosts?* I gave her the only answer I could: *you are dear to me like nobody else ever will be—and they were also you, even if you don't remember them.*

And I know that this is something that will pass: a bit of French dramatics she inherited from her maternal line. *We will either love or hate each other, but we will never be ambivalent, never again*, she herself has said to me before; to that end, we've learned to cook our backups to our own specifications, and to make our own deep linkages to each other's neuroroutines. If, for whatever reason, one of us must be restored, the other will be too. If we die, we die together, and we will be restored either to what we are now, or to what we were years ago, before we had become a *we* in the first place. We will never have to miss each other. I will never have to miss her again.

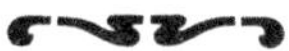

A Song Unheard

Brian T. Hodges

Patrek paused at the top of the gangway, acclimating himself to the sticky, iron-rich air of Malekai station. He ran his hand over the skiff's heavily pitted doorframe—the constant shuttling up-and-down was taking its toll on the little ship. It wouldn't be long before the hull cracked and collapsed. But that was typical in these outposts. Everything here was temporary, only intended to last for as long as the planetoid continued to yield up her ores. Even Patrek's presence was fleeting. He was there to verify accounts for the mining co-op, then move on to the next assignment. There was no time for delay, which was what he wanted. Constant movement kept him one step ahead of himself, safeguarding his anonymity.

Patrek fixed his cap low on his brow, shouldered his duffel bag, and stepped into an explosion of voices echoing off the transport docks' bare metal walls. Words flew by his ears. Fast and staccato. Disorienting. *Language*, Patrek knew. *His language.* But he could make no sense of it. He couldn't hear where one word started and the next ended. He couldn't hear the openness of vowels or the stops of consonants. It was always like this after the long solitude of intersystem travel. And he longed to reacquaint himself with words, mimic their sounds. He wanted to say "hello," to feel the wind and vibration form in his throat then take shape as it passed his teeth and lips. He needed to sense that effortless connection between mind and expression. But the word died in his mouth. He couldn't speak, he shouldn't. Even in this roiling sea of noise, he might be heard and lay bare the shame of his birth.

He pressed into the crowd, fixing his eyes on the ground a few feet ahead of him—a strategy to avoid any unnecessary attempts at conversation. With every step, a small whiteboard slapped against his chest from the end of a tangled lanyard. He was well aware that the board seemed a bit anachronistic, even affected, with all of the datapads and flexscreens available. But technology was always the first thing to shatter in the beat-downs that passed for sport in these remote outposts.

When he arrived at customs, he scribbled a quick note on the board: *Here on business. Couple weeks, at most. Nothing to declare.*

"Pass through." The agent waved him through, barely glancing up from his display screen.

Patrek waited for the buzz and click of the lock release, then exited into the all-too-familiar surroundings. Iron dust had painted the company town in sepia tones. Row upon row of rust-stained apartment blocks spread out before him like the walls of a canyon. The town was identical to the all of the other hastily erected stations he'd visited over the past decade. It was constructed per the preset plans for "a mining outpost supporting 5,000 to 10,000 resident workers with transport to orbital processing and shipping." Towns like Malekai station did not grow organically like the homeworld cities, with all their nonsensical circling avenues or incongruous structures, their strange and wonderful idiosyncrasies. No, company towns were strictly planned communities. The co-ops wasted no effort on character because the station was only meant to stand until the marketable ores were depleted—a process that got quicker and quicker as the extraction operations grew more efficient.

Patrek could have taken a room at one of the corporate apartments near the docks, but those complexes were the social centers of these outposts. He couldn't bear the endless chatter of middle management looking for the next rung in their personal ladder to success, nor could he stand the buzzing of porters and waiters hustling for tips, nor the residents flitting about the lobby bars looking to fill the long empty times that plagued faraway assignments. Patrek took these assignments for the solitude, not to be thrust into a compressed caricature of the homeworlds. So Patrek headed away from the docks, following a caravan of smoke-spewing tractors returning to the mining fields.

The ruts left by their biting treads would lead him to the town's margin, he knew, a place where he wouldn't be tempted to speak. A place inhabited by those who were more broken than he. There, those who were unlucky enough to have survived mining accidents settled into the type of subsistence life that didn't allow for the luxuries of shame and persecution. Patrek had always wondered at how true hunger and desperation seemed to solve the problems that prosperity and free time invited. He wasn't so interested in puzzling out a philosophical answer, as he was in learning to recognize patterns like a rabbit reading an open field for bolt-holes.

Patrek could feel beads of sweat forming on his forehead and dampness spreading across his back. Still, he wore his cap low and his collar up. He quickened his pace. The road out of town was lined with bars, drug theaters, and comfort spas—all teeming with workers trying to forget their days sifting ore from dirt. Patrek had managed to weave his way through the throng until two men, grimy from labor, spilled loudly out of a bar directly in front of him. One of the men, a mix of muscle and fat with bristly hair like a boar, stepped directly into Patrek.

"Eh, pardon me, brutha." The man placed a thick, rust-stained hand on Patrek's shoulder.

Patrek nodded and tried to step aside. The boar blocked him, grabbing a handful of Patrek's coat.

"Are ya' deaf or somethin'?" asked the other man. He was thin as a weed with streams of sweat running down his forehead, leaving grey streaks on his ruddy face. "Max here just apologized t'ya, Ain't ya' got nuthin' t'say?"

Patrek looked up—a mistake. The boar pulled him close. His breath was sour with liquor. The man's eyes widened in disgust as his gaze traced the ridge of pale, fish-like scales that outlined Patrek's brow.

"Oh, feck me," the man shouted, shoving Patrek to the ground. "He's a feckin' castoff." The man took a step back, furiously wiping his hands on his coveralls.

Castoff. Patrek knew a beating was coming. They could've called him anything: half-cast, mule, métis. Any of those would have shown their displeasure. But *castoff* was reserved for disgust, for violence. Patrek scuttled backwards, grabbing for his bag. But just then, a boot drove into his shoulder, pinning him to the hardpan.

"What'ya doin' here, castoff?" The thin man ground his heel into Patrek's collarbone. "Lookin' for yer mama? She's probably workin' the alleys."

"Makes me sick," the boar complained, shaking his head. "It just ain't feckin' right. What's a human doing with one of 'em? It just makes me sick."

A beating was coming. It would go faster if Patrek let them hurt him, if he didn't fight back. So after the first boot connected with his belly, he curled into a ball and took kick after kick until the men were spent and

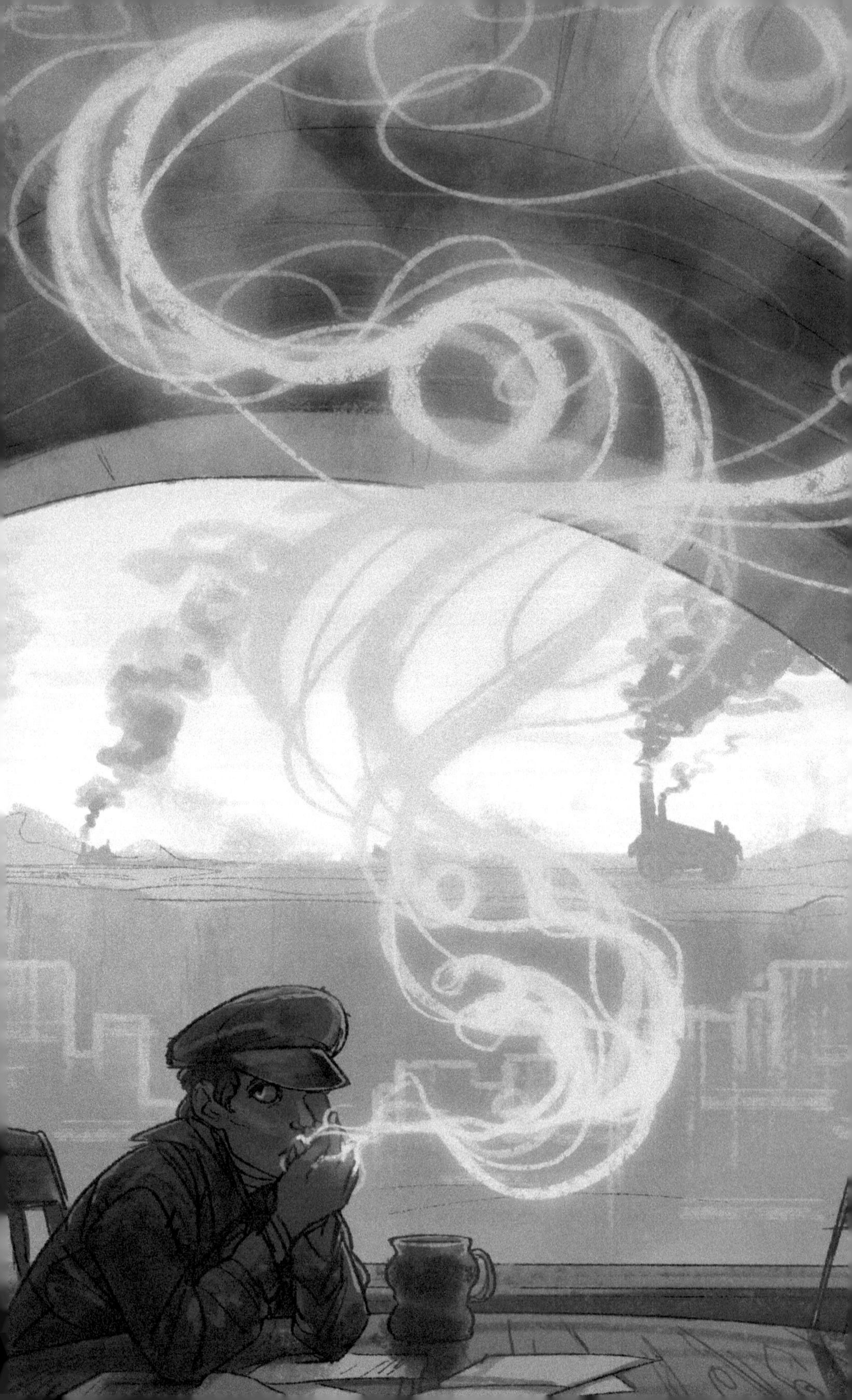

satisfied, a moment that was marked by gobs of spit raining down on him.

He lay in the dirt long after the men left. His mouth tasted coppery with blood, his lips of rust and dirt. Staying put was an act of obeisance. If he rose too soon, the boot boys might return to administer a proper beating. Or others might pick up the chastisement where they had left off. He waited for the interest in his humiliations to wane, for the spectators to drift back to their drink and drugs. Still, he waited longer before stretching his legs, arms, back. Nothing seemed broken; bruises would fade. He moaned involuntarily as he gathered his feet—a sound that began as a deep bass rumble so low as to be barely audible, then grew in volume and pitch like the song of a whale. He caught himself—cursed himself for being unmindful. He could take the beatings, he could take the name calling, but he couldn't let anyone hear his voice.

Patrek looked around to see if anyone had heard him. An old man approached from a storefront, his skin so weathered, so dark and deeply lined, that it looked more like cedar bark than flesh. Patrek wanted to run, but he couldn't catch his breath. He couldn't get away. The man knelt next to him and fixed him with his feral, watery eyes. Patrek tried to turn away, but the old man took a firm hold of his chin and held his face up.

"Shouldn't be here, y'know." The old man's voice sounded like two stones grinding against one another.

Patrek nodded in the man's hand.

"You're more'n a castoff, ain't ya'?"

Patrek looked away, toward the rutted road that would take him away from there.

"You're one of 'em *miracle* babies, no?" The man emphasized the word *miracle* to make it clear that he thought that breeding for new traits was anything but a miracle. "One of 'em freaks that's changin' it all up? Playin' games with nature. Screwin' it all up, if y'ask me."

Patrek fumbled with his whiteboard, shaking and weak. In an unsteady hand, he wrote, *Leaving now. Sorry.*

"It won't go so well next time if you let 'em hear that voice of yours. It's wrong, y'know. Bad enough they're layin' down with 'em, but tryin' t'make things god never intended. That's just plain sick. That's why you've got that voice, y'know—god's punishment."

Patrek nodded again, he'd heard it all before. He looked at the old man and softened his eyes into an apology, a plea. He knew to hide his voice. He had always known. His parents had tried to comfort him, had tried to convince him that his voice was just a sign of evolution speeding up. It was all platitudes—he knew better. It was a fault, a side effect of that generation's utopian daydreaming. It was genetic disinformation. He was lucky, though, that his mark was latent. Unless he spoke, he would only be seen as a castoff. He would be shunned and hated, but not feared. And fear was where the real danger lay. Fear was where beatings crossed the line from punishment to death. So, over the years, he had learned to play the mute. It worked well enough, but he had to be more mindful, more cautious.

"Git you. Git gone, now!"

Patrek followed the ruts until he reached the end of town. There, the tracks disappeared into an endless vista of dirt. Dust plumes interrupted the horizon where massive factory tractors siphoned iron dust from the surface, spewing clouds of waste high into the sky. The noise—rumbling engines, whirring belts, rattling shakers, and screaming drills—carried across the open expanse as a deafening roar. Patrek had found what he was looking for.

A dim light shone from an open doorway. A pungent scent hung around the door, fighting the all-pervasive smell of rust. Lalekeen cuisine, he supposed. His suspicion was confirmed when he heard the chorus of high-pitched chirrups coming from within. Like most of the early arrivals, the insect-like Lalekeen had been broken by years of hard labor. There was no going home for them. Their unpaid transport and medical advances kept them on the stations long after they became useless. Stuck, they eked out subsistence on the edge of society—in large part due to a diet consisting of homeworlder refuse.

Patrek knew that he could relax there. They needed his money, his custom. But they wouldn't bother him; they would barely even notice him. The Lalekeen had never paid much attention to homeworlders, not with ears tuned to chirping.

Days passed and Patrek grew comfortable with his hosts. He settled into a routine, taking over a corner booth for his office, running numbers on his portable, perfectly alone in the middle of a crowd. He downed a drink, two, three. The chirping that had so annoyed him when he first arrived was now a comfort. It was camouflage. And in that hidden place, Patrek felt the urge to speak simmering in his heart. It grew hotter and hotter until it became an urge to sing—an ache he had not felt since childhood. He needed to feel free for just one moment, to remember what it felt like before he learned the word castoff.

He shook his head in frustration, trying to douse the urge. He chastised himself for feeling at ease, for allowing his mind to drift back to the songs that he sang with his mother all those years ago. But still his mind fixated on those long-ago days when he didn't know that his strange voice was anything other than a voice—before he hid his songs in a fog of silence. It took constant fear and tension to maintain his façade, to suppress the need to feel a word form in his mind then slip past his lips—even in places like this where there was no one to hear. The ache grew overwhelming. And finally, Patrek gave in—just a bit. He began to hum a childhood rhyme. Quiet. Tentative. Almost a whisper.

No one heard. No one looked at him.

His body pulsed with excitement. He shivered at the vibration in his throat, the electricity behind his teeth. He grew bolder. He sang a dancing song, sotto voce. Memories poured into his mind—birthdays, family, laughter. A wave of sorrow met primal joy as he shaped words and sounds.

Still, no one heard. He closed his eyes and sang a lament to that lost boy in full voice, allowing the memories to wash over him.

When Patrek opened his eyes, a figure stood before him. The Lalekeen girl was tall with long, thin limbs like a mantis. Her face was a mottled green with orange spots beginning above her compound eyes and sweeping back over her oblong head. She had a scar—more a dent—on the left side of her face. She placed her long hands on the table and leaned into his face. She cocked her head, mandibles twitching. Too close.

Patrek averted his eyes and began to gather his things in clumsy haste. He would return to the docks and take the next shuttle off-world. He could finish his accounts on the transport.

The mantis grabbed his wrist and held it firmly, squeezing harder and harder it until he looked up. With her free hand, she traced figures in the air, signing something. He didn't know what she was trying to say. Patrek's mother had always encouraged him to learn sign language— the last subterfuge of a mute impersonator—but something had kept him from that. He preferred the whiteboard. Somehow it was easier for Patrek to lie when the words were placed on an object and held at a distance.

Sorry. Leaving now. He wrote.

She grabbed his whiteboard and scribbled something on it. Patrek took the board.

I hear you.

Sorry. Leaving now. He pointed at his words.

She wiped Patrek's words from the board and wrote, *No.*

I hear you, here! she continued, taking Patrek's hand and laying it on her sleek chest. She tapped her words with her free hand. *I hear you, here! I hear you, here! I hear you, here!*

Patrek's mouth was dry with panic. He had to run. He had to leave. But the girl was blocking his exit, insistent that he understand something before the inevitable beating would begin.

She pointed at the scar on her head, then wrote. *Ears broken. But I hear you.*

Patrek nodded, hoping to appease her.

She raised her fingers to her mouth and drew them forward and up, then held an open palm to Patrek. She repeated the gesture.

Patrek shook his head and pushed the whiteboard across the small table.

It was song. Beautiful. She wrote, repeating the gesture. *Sing again.*

Patrek shook his head.

"No," he bellowed. The girl cringed, and snatched the whiteboard.

Bad word, she wrote. *Hurt.*

Patrek stared at the whiteboard for several long moments. What was this cruel game? Was she trying to trick him? He was desperate for the isolation that he hated so much, for the self-imposed silence that purchased his solitude, his anonymity. Years of beatings screamed in his mind—leave now! Leave fast! Don't come back! He was overwhelmed by shame, by consciousness. He pushed past the girl and walked determinedly out of the public house, leaving his belongings behind. He didn't look back. He didn't have to. He could feel the girl's eyes follow him to the exit. What did she want from him? Once out of sight, he collapsed onto the dirt, heaving great sobs that were lost to the roar of machines.

After a few moments, he felt a hand grasp his shoulder—a hand that lacked violence. He looked up through red-rimmed eyes to see the girl crouched before him. They sat in silence for a long moment, looking at one another.

Sing again. He recognized her gesture. *Beautiful.*

He shook his head, but did not look away.

She took his hand, cradling it in hers. The girl's twig-like fingers stroked his palm in slow rhythm, as if playing a dreamy arpeggio. She nodded motherly encouragement.

Sing again. Beautiful.

All at once, his tension melted away, leaving behind a deep weariness, a profound loneliness. He looked at her, for the first time truly seeing her. She was beautiful despite her strangeness—perhaps because of it. Her eyes shone like multifaceted garnets. The crown of her head swept back in a graceful and symmetrical curve that reminded Patrek of a gentle ocean swell. Her chitin excreted oils that gave an iridescent glow. Her presence—her radiance—cast a light on him that made it impossible to hide, impossible to feel alone. He wanted to dissolve into the moment, but he knew that he couldn't. He had to leave. He had to disappear.

The girl let go of Patrek's hand and wrote, *Name?* She leaned close to hear him over the machinery.

Patrek spoke his name, two long, low vowels punctuated by clicking stops.

No, not that, she wrote. *That's just a word. Names must tell who you are. You were A-Song-Unheard.*

Patrek nodded.

But I hear you, she wrote. *You have a new name. Tell me who you are.* She leaned in, waiting.

He could smell her spicy breath. He breathed it in, filling himself with her presence, her essence. His cheek brushed her scar and something in him broke like a dam releasing its backwaters. Words spilled past his lips. More words than he had ever spoken. Words he had never tried to form in his mouth. He told her of his life. Of his childhood. Of his mother and father. Of learning of castoffs. Of his voice. Of the beatings. Of the places he'd seen. Of the places he'd left. Of the loneliness that followed him everywhere. Of the hopes he'd drowned just to maintain his solitude.

Not your name. She tapped the words on the board after each story.

Patrek stopped, exhausted, not knowing what she wanted, not

knowing what else to say.

In his silence, he realized that he knew nothing about the girl. "What's your name?"

I am no one. She tapped the dent on her temple then gestured around. *I cannot hear, I have no connection. I am A-Shard-Broken.*

"But you hear me," he said. "That's not your name."

Silence again. The two sat on the ground, nameless, cradling each other's hands.

After a long wait, the girl dropped Patrek's hands and wrote again, *I am part of something.* She gestured a circle on the palm of her hand.

He felt her words work their way under his skin, slip past his mind, and settle in a place so hidden and cold that he shuddered at their warm presence. It was his failing—his voice—that gave the girl her chance at a connection. The dark shame that had driven him across the expanse was her light. He knew he couldn't be that beacon; he was scheduled to depart for his next assignment within the week. And yet, he couldn't leave while her question lingered. Who was he? He considered all of the words that described him. Son? Man? Castoff? Traveler? No. He realized in that moment that he had left all of those words behind. He had reached the end of his travels. He was part of something now, and couldn't return to his path of isolation.

Finally, he looked to the girl's gemstone eyes and said, "I have no name, but I'll find one—we both will. We have all the time in the world." And he knew it to be true because the words were spoken by a mouth that had never learned to lie. The Lalekeen girl also knew it to be true because she heard his words despite broken ears. Newly unnamed, the two leaned into one another, stealing a future from the temporary life of Malekai station.

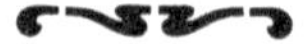

Contributors

Mike Algera has authored three poetry collections: *Old Gods for New*, *Outskirts*, and *Like Indigenous Tiger*. He has been published by *Arc Poetry Magazine*, BareBack Lit, Hamilton Arts & Letters, Nostrovia Poetry, Word Salad, and Cyclamens & Swords Publishing. He lives in Hamilton with his high maintenance dog, Grendel. His favourite themes include dysfunctional families, Oriental mysticism, vigilante justice, love and love in all of the wrong places. His home away from home is in digital la-la land, at www.mikealgera.com.

M. P. Diederich was born somewhere in New England in 1985. Despite his interest in dangerous subjects, he is not currently under FBI surveillance. He studied English and Creative Writing at Fordham University in New York City while seriously considering joining the French Foreign Legion. He currently lives in Brooklyn, where he's trying to introduce more green vegetables into his diet and maybe go for a run every once in a while.

Casey Ellis graduated from Manhattanville College in 2004, where he wrote a senior thesis on ethical issues in Oscar Wilde's *The Picture of Dorian Gray*. He received a Masters in English from the University at Buffalo in 2006, with a thesis on the language of the fool characters in Shakespeare's major tragedies. He is currently an adjunct with the English departments of Westchester Community College and Berkeley College, and a verbal skills tutor with Huntington Learning Center. Whenever possible, Casey updates his literary blog *"Tolle, lege!"* (http://caseyellis66.wordpress.com/). Before becoming the editor of *Startling*

Sci-Fi: New Tales of the Beyond, Casey was the line editor of three previous New Lit Salon Press collections: *Southern Gothic: New Tales of the South*, *Behind the Yellow Wallpaper: New Tales of Madness*, and *Salon Style: Fiction, Poetry & Art* which featured his short story "The Creature from the Lake."

Eve Fisher was adopted from an orphanage in Athens, Greece as a child, and hasn't quit traveling since. She's lived in almost every state in America, worked almost every kind of job, and managed to visit every national park, monument, state park, giant ball of string, and iguana farm west of the Mississippi. In between and during travels, she writes. Eve has been published numerous times in *Alfred Hitchcock Mystery Magazine*, as well as other publications, including "Space & Time." Her website is www.evefishermysteries.wikispaces.com.

Daniel Gooding was born in 1984, and now works as a library assistant at the University of Bristol. He is the author of a novella and a collection of short stories, both unpublished, and is currently working on more. He lives in Bath with his wife and two children.

Rob Hartzell is a graduate of the University of Alabama MFA program. He is currently at work on a story cycle, titled "Pictures of the Floating-Point World," from which "The Dead and Eternal" is taken. Other stories from the cycle have appeared at *Eunoia Review* and *Flyover Country Review*.

Brian T. Hodges lives in the mossy forests of the Pacific Northwest, where he works as a lawyer, researcher, and non-fiction writer. He spends most of his free time exploring the woods, lakes, and creek beds with his Newfoundland dogs. His fiction has been published by *The Strange Edge*, received an Honorable Mention from the Writers of the Future contest (V31 Q1 2014), and was a finalist in the 2013 N3F Amateur Short Story Contest.

David W. Landrum teaches English at Grand Valley State University in Allendale, Michigan. His speculative fiction has appeared widely, his science fiction in *Aphelion, Fiction on the Web, Veterans of Future*

Wars, *Death-Head Grin*, *Roar and Thunder*, and many other journals and anthologies.

Scott Lambridis' debut novel, *The Many Raymond Days*, about a scientist who discovers the end of time, received the 2012 Dana Award and is represented by Richard Florest of Robert Weisbach Creative Management. Stories of his have appeared in *Slice*, *Painted Bride*, *Cafe Irreal*, *Flash Fiction Funny*, *New American Writing*, and other journals. He recently completed his MFA from San Francisco State where he received the Miriam Ylvisaker Fellowship, and three literary awards. Before that, he earned a degree in neurobiology, and co-founded Omnibucket.com, through which he co-hosts the Action Fiction! performance series.

J. P. Lorence is a resident of Vancouver, Canada, who pursues graphite art, spoken word, and occasionally fiction writing.

Stefanie Masciandaro is a New York-based artist with a love of all things fuzzy and sugary, not at the same time though. Sometimes she likes to pretend she looks like an old Renaissance painting. You know, those Italian ones with the great noses. Often she can be found wandering the streets of Manhattan in a slightly dazed state, and will frequently ask questions like "What day is it?" or "Is three cups of coffee in one sitting too many?" or "Yes, but is it feminist?" When not doing those things, she is probably hunched over a laptop working in Photoshop or pretending no one can hear her sing in her studio.

Jhon Sanchez. As Colombian, Mr. Sanchez writes the disgrammatical. Mr. Sanchez hung his three law diplomas above the toilet in his Brooklyn apartment. After surviving his first short story, "Too Funny to Commit Suicide," he went on to study writing at Long Island University. His work has been featured in *Brooklyn Paramount* and *The Overpass*. This September, Mr. Sanchez is going to be a resident at the Edward Albee Foundation in Montauk, NY (No visitors allowed!). He would like to thank Samuel Ferri, Orlando Ferrand, Martha Hughes, Barbara Wallace, Alexander Saenz, and Nan Frydland for their editorial comments, as well as Lewis Warsh, Don Scotti, Mom, the Jamaican Lady next door, and the keys left by the Brazilian.

Adam Sass is a writer of gay-themed, suspenseful sci-fi. In addition to self-publishing a collection of comedic essays, *A Look at the Great Gay Tipping Point*, he blogs monthly LGBT pop culture op-eds at StayOnFountain.com. He lives in West Hollywood with his nurse husband and dachshund. Keep up with what he's drinking on his (over) active Twitter @TheAdamSass.

Marcus S. Robin is a Fraud Analyst residing in the Mile High City of Denver, CO where some believe the unusually high occurrence of UFO sightings is attributable to the elevation, while others believe it's due to the recreational marijuana. He's okay with either theory.

Charlotte Unsworth lives in West Yorkshire, England. She has published several short stories as e-books, and is currently completing a novel. Connect with her on Twitter @lotti_brown or at www.charlotteunsworth.com.

About NLSP

We are New Lit Salon Press and we create books. We are writers. We are artists. We are makers with a mission: to publish the best and brightest, to amplify the voice of a generation lost in the void of a system concerned only about million dollar bestsellers. We look to the past but move boldly towards the future.

Founded by Brian Centrone (Publisher) and Jordan M. Scoggins (Creative Director) in 2012, New Lit Salon Press is based on the principle that Words and Art can and should coexist. NLSP is committed to publishing essays, stories, poems, novels, and art from undiscovered writers and promising artists who struggle to thrive in a marketplace that fails to recognize their talent. We believe in what you do.

The world of publishing is changing. NLSP not only recognises that but embraces it. To meet the demands of the evolving marketplace, NLSP releases are available on all major ebook platforms. However, because we are suckers for the printed page and we love the artistry of a physical object, we also produce print-on-demand trade editions of select titles.

With over 20 collective years of experience in creative, publishing, technology, and academic fields, we bring a unique skill set to the table. Our comprehensive approach is designed to nurture new and unheard talent in ways most indie publishers do not. We love what we do (and hope you do too).

We are artists. We are writers. We are NLSP and we create books.